**HIS ARMS WENT AROUND HER AND HIS
EYES RESTED ON HER SWEET,
SENSUOUS LIPS. . . .**

"I know I have no right to interfere in your life. I just
. . . can't help myself."

Matt kissed her waiting lips ever so gently, lingering like
a velvet whisper on her yearning, sensitive soul. Yielding
to the curve of his strong arms, the solid fortress of his
chest, the solace of his healing kiss, Kathryn surrendered
to her desire. This was where she belonged—where she
wanted to be all along—in his arms . . . knowing his
passion . . . responding to his kiss . . . and then she stopped
herself as if she were a person about to plunge off a preci-
pice. *Oh, God!* she thought. *No! How could I?*

A CANDLELIGHT ECSTASY ROMANCE ®

KINDLE THE FIRES

Tate McKenna

A CANDLELIGHT ECSTASY ROMANCE ®

Published by
Dell Publishing Co., Inc.
1 Dag Hammarskjold Plaza
New York, New York 10017

Dell ® TM 681510, Dell Publishing Co., Inc.

Candlelight Ecstasy Romance®, 1,203,540, is a registered
trademark of Dell Publishing Co., Inc., New York, New
York.

ISBN: 0-440-14506-6

Printed in the United States of America
First printing—May 1983

To Rita,
for her inspiration and encouragement;
friendship and long lunches.

To Our Readers:

We have been delighted with your enthusiastic response to Candlelight Ecstasy Romances® and we thank you for the interest you have shown in this exciting series.

In the upcoming months we will continue to present the distinctive sensuous love stories you have come to expect only from Ecstasy. We look forward to bringing you many more books from your favorite authors and also the very finest work from new authors of contemporary romantic fiction.

As always, we are striving to present the unique, absorbing love stories that you enjoy most—books that are more than ordinary romance.

Your suggestions and comments are always welcome. Please write to us at the address below.

Sincerely,

The Editors
Candlelight Romances
1 Dag Hammarskjold Plaza
New York, New York 10017

CHAPTER ONE

"No, Hal, I've made a decision, and I'm going to stick to it." Kathryn shook her head and paced the now-empty room. "There is nothing more for me here, and I want to make a complete break with the past." She stopped to gaze out one of the floor-to-ceiling windows that flanked the brick fireplace. Her eyes traveled from the gold-leafed oaks which graced the sloping backyard to the flagstone patio to the stocky red brick barbeque pit. It was handsome and sturdy-looking, but Kathryn knew it was flawed. It didn't draw smoke up the chimney like it should, but always billowed white clouds into the face of the cook. And several bricks had been chopped into splintered hunks to make the whole thing level on top. But, *they* had made it. It had taken the better part of a month one summer, but *they* had finished it together. Now, someone else would be using it. Kathryn sighed heavily.

Hal's firm voice interrupted her thoughts. "Well, you're sure as hell going overboard! Sometimes I wonder if you've lost your reasoning, Kathryn. You don't have to leave the entire country to break away. Stay close by and let me set you up in a nice apartment on Pennsylvania or DuPont Avenue. Or, if you want more room, we'll find something for you near Kennett Square or Newark. That way, I can keep an eye on you. I'll take care of you. And I'll see that you have a good job. Emery would have appreciated that." His voice was gentle at the end, but Kathryn was in no mood for sentimentality.

Viewing the house one more time was bad enough. If she let down her guard at all, her restored emotional facade would crumble. She might even change her mind. Sharply, she replied, "Don't tell me what Emery would have wanted! I . . . I can only deal with what is happening in my life . . . now! And what I want to do is to get out. Now that the house is sold, the bills paid, I want . . . need . . . to start another life, somewhere else. I want to be where nothing reminds me of Emery. Can you understand that, Hal?"

He shook his head. "I just hope you aren't making a mistake by going so far away. I think you're still bitter because Emery left you with a mountain of bills and barely enough assets to cover them." Hal's tone was honest and he looked at her with clear blue eyes. He knew her well. Hal had been their lawyer, their business adviser, and their friend. And afterward, he had tried to take care of Kathryn, but she just wouldn't let him. She had insisted on making all the decisions by herself.

Kathryn placed her hands on her slim hips. "Well, you'd think, as smart as he was, he'd plan better than he did!" She covered her face with slender hands, instantly regretting her words. "Oh, God—what am I saying, Hal? You don't plan to die of a heart attack at forty-two!" She raised her head, and there were no tears. She had cried them all out long ago. "He . . . he did okay. We had a marvelous life together, and now, I *have* managed to pay

12

everything off. I still have a small nest egg . . . and the Texas property."

She pushed her thick hair back from her delicate oval face. In the evening shadows that crept through the empty house, her hair appeared as a dark mane, cascading to her shoulders. Hal couldn't see the auburn highlights or detect the usual sparkle in her chestnut-brown eyes, but he knew they were there. For a while, the sparkle, the zest for life, was gone. But, in the past few months, more of her old enthusiasm had reappeared. Now, she had this crazy idea to move to Texas—and was adamant about it.

"Kathryn, you don't even know anything about that place."

She shrugged. "I know that Emery's uncle lived there until a few years ago. So it's habitable."

Hal's blue eyes softened with tenderness. "Kathryn, why don't you just go for a visit? Wait before you make that final decision. I'll help you. If you will accept nothing else, at least I can give you support."

"We've been all through this before. Let's not rehash it again." Kathryn was fully aware that Hal was sincere in his offers to help. He had been a good friend of hers during the eight years of her marriage to Emery. And his friendship with Emery went back further than that. Kathryn knew she could trust Hal and rely on him, but she was determined to become independent now.

"Hal, I appreciate your concern for me. But it's been a year since he died, and it's time I went out on my own. It's something I must do." She looked at her friend, searching for some kind of understanding.

What she saw was a distinguished-looking man with graying hair and sharp blue eyes. He was trim in his conservative dark suit and tie with the lean physique of an habitual jogger. Hal was of the old school that believed a man should take care of a woman and solve all of her

13

problems. And Kathryn had accepted those same rules. She had let Emery take care of her during their eight-year marriage. And see what had happened to her? Oh, it had been fine for a while. It had been so easy, with him a full fourteen years older than she. Then, a year ago, he died—suddenly and tragically. Kathryn was left totally in control of her life, whether she wanted it or not. And she was inadequately prepared for it. Now she was determined that wouldn't happen again; neither the dependence, nor the helplessness.

Hal looked out the same window and across the yard. As he walked back through the echoing room, he exclaimed futilely, "But Texas, Kathryn! Oh, God, Texas! There's nothing out there but cows and tumbleweed and . . . cowboys! It's crude country, Kathryn. You'll hate it!"

She smiled warmly, her eyes dark and wise. "Well, then, that's what I intend to find out. And, with a wonderful friend like you here, Hal, I can always come back to Delaware if I need to."

And then, as if it were the most natural thing in the world, he bent and kissed her lips. For the first time ever, in all the years she had known him, their lips met and his arms wrapped around her, purposefully and intentionally. And it seemed perfectly natural.

Suddenly they weren't two old and dear friends bidding farewell but a lonely man and a saddened woman accepting each other, mutually searching for affection, perhaps for love.

Hal's lips were caressing and comfortable, not passionate and demanding. They lingered sweetly, allowing time to enjoy and savor. Kathryn yielded to his touch, but in the far recesses of her mind, she wondered why. They had been together often through the years, but had never been drawn to kiss.

She breathed deeply of his light cologne and was re-

14

minded of another time they had been close enough for her to smell his expensive fragrance. It was a Sunday afternoon sail on the Chesapeake Bay, and there were four of them. As friends will do, she had shared her beer with him, and he had let her steer the boat. She had braced against his shoulder for support while the damp wind whipped vigorously at her. It dried on her skin, giving the beer a salty taste as they exchanged the can. She had breathed that same cologne, mingled with brackish air that day, but had never actually tasted his lips, had never desired it.

And yet, this moment seemed so natural, almost expected.

Then, just as abruptly as it swept in, the salty wind died down and the mist that enshrouded them blew away. They were once again two people standing in the quiet of an empty, almost-dark house, bidding farewell to each other, and the past, and, regrettably now, the future.

He moved away from her and muttered softly, "My God, Kathryn, I . . . I didn't mean to—" He stopped abruptly, his voice thick and hoarse.

Her eyes smiled in the darkness. "Don't apologize, Hal. It was wonderful." *Was it wonderful?* she asked herself. *Was it, really?*

"Kathryn, don't go. I think we could make it."

Why now? Why are you doing this to me now, Hal? Why not earlier? Why not last week? Oh, Lord, I know why not! I wouldn't let you! I wouldn't let you—or me—until now, when it was safe. When I knew I would be leaving.

"I must go, Hal. You know that."

He smiled faintly, acknowledging. His hand rested quite naturally on her shoulder, not seeking her hair or the warmth of her nape. His left hand sought her right one and brought it to his lips. He turned her fingers so that his mouth touched the sensitive tips. Again, his lips were warm and sweet and caring.

"If you ever need anything, Kathryn, I'll be there. Just call." He pressed her hand to his lips again. "Promise me you'll call if you get in trouble."

Kathryn's eyes glistened as she nodded, whispering, "I will, Hal. I will."

And she turned toward the door, thinking about his kiss, his promise. It was reassuring and comfortable and, yes, wonderful. And yet, it was a kiss she could walk away from . . . and remember.

White Queen Anne's lace hugged the fence rails near the roadside, accenting green rolling fields beyond. As the fields gave way to forest, red sumac edged the road and blazed against the yellow-leafed sweet gums and emerald pines. This autumn brilliance flashed by quickly as the sporty blue Corvette sped through the eastern Texas country-side.

Kathryn Coleman pursued her course with singular determination. Her mouth was set in a thin line and the muscles in her slim body were taut with anticipation. Hal's predictions were half-right. There were a few cows grazing peacefully, but not a tumbleweed in sight. And cowboys—who cared? Certainly not Kathryn! In fact, she was indifferent to this glorious manifestation of her environment. She had but one goal: to end her three-day trip from Delaware and arrive at her destination, her new life.

She pondered about the house and property that would be her home. Emery had mentioned it, having spent summers at his uncle's small farm as a boy. But Kathryn had never been there. They had just kept the property, paid taxes on it yearly, and arranged for neighbors, the Chandlers, to keep the land mowed. It entailed an exchange of communication and money several times a year. As usual,

Emery had taken care of it. When he died, it was necessary for Kathryn to liquidate everything. She had tried to sell the Texas property. However, of all the assets, it was the only thing that hadn't sold. Now, as she traveled toward the small town, she could understand why there wasn't even an offer on the place. She wasn't exactly in the heart of a thriving metropolis. Who would want to live out here? Wryly, she answered her own question. *Who, indeed? Just me—a woman learning to be independent. No,* she corrected determinedly. *Being independent!*

Anxious to speed up the process, Kathryn leaned forward impatiently and pressed firmly on the accelerator. The end—or rather, her new beginning—was nearly in sight. The next rise revealed a sharp curve in the road ahead. Instinctively, Kathryn fought for control of the low sports car as it rapidly entered the turn. She tried to touch the brakes lightly, but heard the whine of tires as the back of her car skidded across the width of the road. With a muffled cry, she realized that a car loomed ahead, aimed directly at her as she ricocheted across both lanes. The loud screech of brakes filled her head, blocking out all thoughts as she subconsciously waited to hear the crunch of metal and glass. With a shuddering gust of wind, the large vehicle brushed past, missing her Corvette by inches!

Kathryn breathed a jerky sigh as she realized that she had not been hit. The rush of blood pounded in her ears and pulsed wildly through her body, leaving her visibly shaking. She allowed the car to roll slowly to the side of the road, finally stopping of its own accord.

An angry masculine voice penetrated her distraught emotional state. "What is hell do you think you're doing, lady? You must have been flying around that curve! You almost got yourself killed—and me, too!"

Kathryn didn't even look up at the man who railed at her from the Cadillac. He had every right to be mad. She had almost ended it for both of them! She was very frightened, but just couldn't face him. Without thinking, she pressed the accelerator hard and sped away.

His blue eyes narrowed as the navy-blue Corvette with white racing stripes disappeared from sight. He was offered only a fleeting glance of the lovely oval face with large, frightened, dark eyes and burnt copper hair billowing in the wind . . . but he was intrigued.

Kathryn's first week in her new home was punctuated by a typical, Texas-style event. Barbeque! She tried to concentrate on the man before her. He looked like a typical Texas politician . . . beige western-cut suit, lizard cowboy boots, and gray hair visible under the tall stetson hat. His Texas drawl resounded above the twangy sounds of a small band playing country music.

"I was in Delaware once, Mrs. Coleman . . . ah, Kathryn. May I call you Kathryn?"

"Yes, of course," she nodded impartially. There was nothing specific about Gilbert Ashland that Kathryn disliked. It was generally everything about him! In all fairness, though, perhaps it was the occasion, not the man. Nan and Davis Chandler, her closest neighbors, had insisted that she attend the political rally they were hosting. It was loud and boisterous and not at all the kind of event she enjoyed. She wondered why she had allowed Nan to persuade her to come.

"As I was saying, we went to Delaware once, and stayed at the . . . ah . . . the big hotel on the square . . . the ah . . ."

"DuPont Hotel," Kathryn filled in indifferently.

"Ah, yes, the DuPont Hotel . . . lovely place, wasn't it, Lilly?"

Lilly turned insipid eyes toward Kathryn. "Ye-as, it was simply lovely." Her sweet, syrupy drawl sounded like a bad actress in a movie about the South. It was the first time Kathryn had ever heard the word "yes" spoken with two syllables.

Gil continued. "There is so much history in that little state with all those signers of the Declaration of Independence and it being the first state to ratify the Constitution. It gives you a marvelous sense of Americanism just to be there, walking the brick streets of old New Castle!"

Kathryn smiled indulgently at Gil's history lesson, half expecting rockets to explode behind his graying head and the band to break into "The Star-Spangled Banner." Instead, it played "The Yellow Rose of Texas" and the mayor's handsome countenance remained poised. His statements brought into focus the contrast of her past with the present, and she glanced down with an inner smile at her own western appearance. Hal would probably tease her, in his subtle way, about the plaid shirt and jeans she had purchased for the event.

Turning her attention back to Gil, she asked, "Did you get a chance to attend the horse races?"

However, that was touchy political territory, especially in Texas, so Gil avoided answering by ignoring Kathryn's question altogether. "You know, Kathryn, here in Texas, our heritage is much more recent than in Delaware. But we've fought our share of battles for independence. And we have our heroes. Did you know that Twin Oaks sent three men to the battle of the Alamo? Of course, Texas lost many heroes there. But some were made, too. Take Sam Houston, for instance. He once slept here, when he was running for office. That was when this town was a thriving agricultural center. Then, the railroad bypassed us and took in Dallas instead. Otherwise, we might have been the prosperous metropolis of the West that Dallas is!"

"Oh, Gil, you sound like you're regretful." Gil's wife,

Lilly, scowled sweetly. "I like Twin Oaks just the way it is . . . small and . . . cozy."

Nosy is probably a better word, thought Kathryn sarcastically.

Lilly's drawl continued. "Kathryn, de-ah, have you ev-ah been he-ah, to Texas? I don't recall your visiting Twin Oaks befo-ah."

Kathryn smiled indulgently at the only woman who hadn't worn slacks or jeans to the casual affair. Attired in a wispy, flowing voile dress covered with pink and lavender flowers, Lilly Ashland was the essence of femininity.

"No, Mrs. Ashland, I've never been to Texas before. This is my first experience in the West. And, I must say, I'm surprised. I expected cactus and tumbleweeds, but Twin Oaks is very lush."

The Southern drawl seemed to thicken. "My de-ah, why ev-ah did you decide to come out he-ah to this wild country by yourself?"

Kathryn gazed mildly at the serene, green-sloping eastern Texas farmland that surrounded them. She'd be damned if she'd admit to this probing couple her real reasons for coming out to Texas—that she was broke and there was no alternative if she wanted to be independent. There was only one way to shut them up. And it was partially true.

"Actually, my husband and I had discussed a trip west before he died. Coming here alone was not my choice. But I think this is a good place to start my new life."

"Oh, my de-ah, I know you are just floundering in life without your husband, and I didn't mean to—"

Gilbert Ashland moved closer. "What Lilly means is that she can't imagine anyone doing anything so brave and courageous as you are doing, Kathryn. We are proud to have you in our community."

"Thank you, Mayor Ashland," she murmured.

20

He took her hand and held it while he spoke. "Gil. Please call me Gil. I hope you won't forget that we're now your new friends and will be glad to help you any time you need it." He applied a light pressure to her hand as he said the words *friends* and *help*. It was very discreet, but slightly unnerving.

A feminine voice interrupted. "More iced tea, Kathryn?"

Gratefully, Kathryn nodded at Nan Chandler, hostess of the barbeque.

Nan smiled knowingly and motioned to the dark-haired boy who trailed her with a huge pitcher, filling tea glasses. She leaned close to her newest guest's side. "Are you sure you don't want a beer, Kathryn?"

Casting a brief, longing glance at the choices, she declined. "Tea will be fine, thank you, Nan."

Wisely, Nan detected the desperation in Kathryn's expression and offered, "Would you like to help me, Kathryn? It will give you a chance to mingle among the crowd."

"Yes! I'd love to!" Kathryn moved quickly away from the power of Gilbert Ashland and his inquisitive wife. She knew instinctively that these were people to watch out for and stay away from, if possible. She would make it a point to manage in Twin Oaks without their help.

Kathryn followed Nan through the casually attired crowd which was gathered in bunches around the beer kegs or the huge grill where Davis Chandler, Nan's husband, hovered over great slabs of meat. She couldn't avoid contrasting this event with her former life in Delaware. This Texas barbeque was like another world where the speech, as well as the dress, was alien. Kathryn admired Nan as she mingled easily with the crowd. It seemed like a monumental task to host a political event in your own backyard, yet Nan and Davis handled it smoothly. It was

21

as if entertaining was a way of life for them. Yes, living in Texas was going to be a change for Kathryn—and a challenge. But she needed that.

"Help, Davis!" Nan grinned, sidling close to her husband. "Rescue Kathryn from the clutches of your favorite mayor! He and Lilly had her cornered, and you promised to help me keep an eye on them."

Davis frowned and moved away from the heat of the huge grill. "I hope you don't think we're all like that, Kathryn. There are some very nice folks in Twin Oaks. Have you met everyone here?" His gaze scanned the crowd and searched the driveway lined with vehicles before returning to the two women beside him.

"Nan introduced me to most." Kathryn nodded.

"But the Ashlands latched onto her and you know why! Gil recognizes a beautiful woman and poor Lilly is so nosy—"

"Don't worry, you two," Kathryn said with a laugh. "I can take care of myself with the Ashlands." *Who's doing the talking here? The new Kathryn? Absolutely!* she thought proudly.

"I'm sure you can. But they are rather obnoxious at times." Davis smiled grimly. "The Ashlands are part of the reason for this political rally, you know. We intend to present both sides in this election by offering the residents of Twin Oaks an opponent to their incumbent mayor for the first time in years. As soon as he arrives . . ." An annoying glance exchanged between Nan and Davis.

"He'll be here soon," Nan assured them. "Where there's food—"

Davis motioned restlessly with a thick strong hand that was wrapped around a beer. "Yeah, well, he has more responsibility now than just food. Where in the hell—"

"Davis, please!"

"All right, all right!" He sighed and turned to Kathryn

22

with a change of subject. "What do you think of Twin Oaks?"

"Twin Oaks was a rather pleasant surprise, but I like it. And I love your ranch, Davis. It's beautiful out here."

Davis's chest puffed with pride. "You're not only beautiful, Kathryn. You're intelligent, too!" He gazed anxiously toward the driveway, then quickly back to the party. Davis was a large, barrel-chested man with reddish-sandy hair covering his massive arms and curling around the open neck of his western shirt. But for all his brawn, he exuded a gentleness that made Kathryn feel instantly at ease.

"And you're astute to notice," Kathryn quipped, good-naturedly.

His eyes rested gently on Kathryn. "We want you to feel right at home here, Kathryn."

Her brown eyes softened as she smiled. "Thank you, Davis. I'm beginning to feel at home already." How could she tell him that she really wanted to be left alone to adjust to her new life-style? She didn't want to meet people or go places. They couldn't imagine how dissimilar this Texas life-style was to the familiar customs she left in Delaware. This wasn't home at all . . .

"Excuse me, Kathryn. I think our candidate is here," Davis muttered. As he made his way toward the driveway, she could hear him grumbling under his breath, "It's about damn time . . ."

Her eyes followed him to the silver and gray Cadillac that had pulled to a stop near the rambling ranch house. She wondered briefly why the car seemed vaguely familiar, but quickly dismissed the thought and turned to the sound of Mayor Ashland's silver-toned voice.

"Excuse us, ladies. Excuse us, please. I must go meet my competitor!" He smiled congenially and guided his wife ahead of him through the crowd.

An immediate exclamation of awe rose from the guests as they surged, en masse, toward the newcomer with Davis. They gathered about to shake hands and talk, completely hiding the candidate from view. Abruptly, they were parted, politely but firmly, by the mayor, who aimed to make an occasion of the meeting. Masculine hands shook in an exhibition of friendly competition and suddenly, out of nowhere, a flashbulb flared from the crowd. Several bursts of light perpetuated the meeting and the tone for the evening was set. The event was political, and Mayor Gilbert Ashland was obviously taking advantage.

Nan's excited voice broke into Kathryn's observations. "Come on, Kathryn. I want to introduce you to Matt. He used to be a professional football player!"

Kathryn looked doubtful. "And now he's the candidate for mayor?"

Nan smiled indulgently. "Sure. Football player turned small-town politician. Sounds like a B-grade movie, doesn't it?" Nan giggled.

"Sounds smart to me. He's already recognized. That's half the battle."

Nan shook her head. "Half the battle is getting this dude to take it seriously. Matt's heart just isn't in this race. He's only running because Davis asked him to. They're coconspirators in this operation. Come on."

Puzzled but curious, Kathryn allowed herself to be pulled by Nan through the enthusiastic crowd until they stood before him. Kathryn looked up at the huge, muscular man, this near-celebrity, and almost laughed. He was taller than Davis Chandler, with well-defined shoulders and arms. And yet, he was draped over two matchstick-like crutches, dwarfing them as he did everything and everyone near him. Her eyes traveled upward to his face where she beheld the squared jawline, tanned complexion, sapphire-blue eyes, and blond curly hair. His eyes gripped hers for a moment and something intangible passed between them. An electric smile beamed at her.

"Well, hel-lo, gorgeous! Nice to meet you. Don't go away. I want to get to know you later." Matt Logan's voice was smooth and enticing.

Speechless for a moment at his rather brash come-on, Kathryn stared up at him, finally muttering, "What an interesting candidate for mayor you'll make, Mr. Logan." She had not been so affected by the physical presence of a man in years, and she felt very young and foolish.

He pressed her slim hand into his, submerging it completely. "The pleasure is mine, I can assure you." There was something sensuous about the way he spoke to her, touched her.

Then he was gone to the next outstretched hand. Even as his powerful hand left hers for the next one, Kathryn felt his warm energy radiate through her palm. He was magnetic . . . and presumptuous. What had he said to her? *I want to get to know you later.* The nerve of him! Why, he didn't know anything about her! What if . . . she were married? It probably didn't matter to him!

She couldn't take her eyes off him as he kindled the crowd with his voltaic charm. Could smiling and shaking hands have such an effect on people? They swarmed after him like kids after the Pied Piper! Actually, he looked incongruous as the two crutches supported his huge frame. One knee was wrapped in an Ace bandage, visible because the leg of his jeans was cut off above the injury. *Ridiculous! That's what this is! Ridiculous! I've been taken by a celebrity! And a football star, at that! How Hal would scoff* . . .

Finally, Kathryn tore her eyes away from him, forcing herself to look in another direction, hoping her thoughts would follow. But her mind raced back to the man, to Matt Logan, to that smile . . . even as she watched the band and dancers intently. She had not been so intrigued by the physical aspects of a man since . . . well, long before Emery. *Before Emery.* Suddenly she felt guilty, like a traitor—a traitor to their love. But she couldn't seem to control her thoughts—and they were only simple, curious thoughts. Was that so strange? Nothing could dislodge the memories. And yet . . . this man . . . Matt . . .

The loud clanging of a wrought-iron triangle brought everyone's attention to Davis, who announced that the long-awaited food was ready. A never-ending table was covered with a checkered tablecloth and loaded with food. It was a Texas feast prepared for the celebration as two political gladiators sparred in the small rural community. It was an opportunity for fun and food, no matter what your political persuasion. Everyone helped himself to potato salad, spiced beans, pickles, jalapeño peppers, thick slices of homemade bread, barbequed pork ribs, and generous slices of barbequed beef brisket.

Kathryn filled her plate and decided to slip away from the crowd. She found a rough stone seat located under a twisted cedar. She could eat alone and . . . think. She was still shaken by her own naive reaction to Matt Logan. Later, from her sheltered view, Kathryn watched the two mayoral candidates' speeches.

The incumbent mayor was at home before the crowd. Gilbert Ashland played them cleverly, succinctly. There were a couple of family-type jokes, a few compliments for individuals in the crowd, and a brief, positive message.

His competition may have been a professional on the gridiron, but not behind the podium. Matt Logan was not as familiar with the dynamics of crowds, how to bring them along, how to influence and excite, how to manipulate. He was blatantly honest and yet managed to leave the crowd with a feeling of admiration for this man who had agreed to oppose the influential mayor—and on crutches, no less. Maybe sympathy was his tactic, Kathryn surmised.

Finally bored with the small-town drama unfolding before her, Kathryn decided it was time to make her exit. The speeches had ended, the crowd again milled noisily, and the band struck up a favorite country tune. Kathryn rose to leave.

"So, there you are!" A magnificent masculine voice rent the air.

Kathryn looked up, slightly startled that anyone had found her so tucked away from the crowd. Yet, there he stood—captivating eyes, winning smile, crutches, and all! His sapphire-blue eyes twinkled merrily, and he was obviously delighted at his discovery. She caught her breath as Matt Logan made his way toward her, his uneven gait perpetuated by the crutches.

"I thought I told you not to disappear, gorgeous. Now, how did you expect me to find you hiding way out here?" His voice was mellow, slightly teasing, slightly rebuffing.

"I didn't," Kathryn lied casually. "It was not my concern that you find me. Believe it or not, I really don't care what your instructions were."

"Well, well, a little snippy, aren't we?" His eyes absorbed her rich auburn hair, mahogany eyes, her sensuous, sassy mouth. "Are you trying to tell me something? If so, speak right up. Don't hold back."

She shrugged, her smoky brown eyes meeting his burning blue gaze. "I'm trying to tell you as subtly as possible that I'm unimpressed with a football star.

"Something tells me you've dropped the subtlety. Fortunately I don't take 'no' easily, especially when an attractive lady is involved." He eased his huge frame down on the bench near her, tugging lightly on her arm until she joined him. "Now, what was your name again? Kathy?"

Kathy? "Kathryn. Kathryn Coleman," she sniffed.

27

"Well, Kathryn Coleman, I'm Matt Logan. And I'm no football star, as you claimed. It happens that I was fool enough to play the game for profit, but that's in the past now. Can we converse on an even level, say local politician to lovely lady?"

Kathryn breathed uneasily. This wasn't exactly what she'd anticipated from him. "Perhaps. If you drop the 'gorgeous dame' routine, I might be willing to listen."

He spread his hands. "Done! Now, how about if I take you away from all this, and we can talk quietly somewhere."

"I think we can say all we need to say right here."

"You know, Kathryn, I certainly didn't expect to find someone as lovely as you here. I'm very impressed. Couldn't we go somewhere for a cup of coffee or a Coke?" There was an easy, self-assuredness about his manner and a marvelous hint of a Texas drawl in his speech. It wasn't overpowering, but it was there.

Her unexpected laughter hurdled the stiff barrier between them. "At least you're honest in your intentions, Matt Logan."

"Aren't you?" His brows raised above the bluest eyes Kathryn had looked into in a long time.

"Yes, very. And, quite honestly, I was about to leave. Alone."

His large hand grasped her slim forearm and warmth radiated from his simple touch. "Then, let's go together."

"No!" Her answer was too quick.

"Why? I come highly recommended. Nan wanted me to meet you and I promised."

"So, you knew me, after all."

He shrugged. "I knew about you. A little. She said you just moved here from Delaware. And you're very beautiful . . . that's my own deduction, Kathryn."

28

She smiled tightly. "Thank you. But, even with your good recommendation, I prefer to leave alone."

"Then let's talk here."

"Look, Matt, I don't mean to be unfriendly, but we have very little in common. Just tell Nan that you tried."

"I don't report to Nan. She knows better than to try to pair me with anyone. She just thought you were an interesting lady. And now that I've met you, so do I."

"I didn't come here searching for someone to take me away from all this. Anyway, that phrase is a bit overused, don't you think?"

His eyes assessed her. "Why did you come here?"

"I couldn't refuse Nan's invitation gracefully."

He grinned. "Back to Nan again. But why did you choose Texas? Are you familiar with this area?"

"Not really. The property belonged to my husband." She moved just enough to loosen his grip on her arm. "It's actually very pretty here. I expected tumbleweeds and cactus and . . . cowboys. Certainly not professional football players who are running for mayor!"

"Ex-pro player," he corrected her, raising one eyebrow.

"Is that why you're an 'ex'?" she asked, motioning to his bandaged leg. "What happened? Did someone tackle you too low?"

He nodded with a grim smile. "Once too often. The last time resulted in my being forced into early retirement. Imagine that, thirty-five and almost over the hill!" He chuckled at his predicament, but Kathryn detected a bitterness underlying his light comments.

"Surely you expected to retire from football at a fairly young age."

"Oh, sure, I knew it was coming. I just . . . I guess I didn't expect or want it to come so soon. I wanted it on my own terms . . . my own time. But things don't always

29

work out that way, do they?" He shifted, struggling to sit comfortably.

Kathryn sighed, thinking of her own life. "No, things don't always work out the way we plan. I hope you don't mind my saying so, Matt, but you look very uncomfortable."

He grimaced and straight white teeth flashed against his golden tanned face. "I guess I've reached my limit of exertion today. My surgery was less than a week ago, and I'm not up to par yet."

Kathryn's brown eyes met his blue ones for a moment as she implored, "Less than a week? Then, why are you here?"

He shrugged. "I had to be here tonight. This political mess Davis got me involved with required my presence. Otherwise, the mayor would have had this captive audience all to himself. As it was, he may as well have."

"You just need some . . . uh, political guidance," she suggested mildly.

"Like speech lessons and a quick course in political systems of Texas!" he said with a laugh.

"No, like studying the issues," she answered honestly.

He considered her statement. "You believe in hitting hard, don't you?"

"Honest, remember?" She tempered her words with a smile.

He rested an elbow on the good knee and looked out across the fields, shaking his head. "I don't know why I let Davis persuade me to get into this insane . . ." Suddenly his blue eyes turned to her boldly. "But enough about me. I'd like to know about you, Kathryn. Why don't we leave here and go over to my place? We could have a drink and relax a little."

Instantly, Kathryn stiffened. He was making another pass at her, after she thought she had made herself perfectly clear. Except for Hal's brief kiss before her departure, she hadn't been approached by a man in the year she had been a widow. In Delaware, she had lived in a sheltered world where everyone knew her and Emery and, even after his death, she had been protected. Hal and other friends made sure of it.

Her brown eyes shot daggers at him as she flushed under his bold gaze. "Matt, you and I have very little in common, and I do not care to go to your place."

"Does that mean you've sworn off socializing altogether? Or that you just don't want to be with me?" His barb drove into her.

She answered him just as sharply. "I've had my share of socializing. But not anything you would enjoy, I'm sure!" She started to walk away, annoyed with this brazen man, and with herself for letting him fluster her.

His warm hand grasped her arm firmly before she could get out of reach. "How do you know what I enjoy? Look— you don't have to be so huffy. I just offered a little friendship—something you seem to be lacking—not a fast romp in bed. I'm hardly up to that, anyway, with my leg in a damn cast!"

Kathryn burned from her neck up and attempted to pull away from his firm grip. "Let me go! Apparently, we're after completely different goals. I'm just looking for a new life, not someone to pick me up!"

He released her arm with a jerk. "Well, you don't have to worry about that! No one in his right mind would want to take off with a frigid iceberg like you!"

Kathryn wheeled away, furious with his words and what this man had done to her. Her reactions to him were inane and infuriatingly immature. And now, she just wanted to escape his presence.

Matt watched her hips move temptingly as she swung

angrily in the opposite direction. Damn! She was a good-looking woman! Spirited, but beautiful!

Seeking her hosts, Kathryn thanked Nan and Davis for the evening and slipped away from the gaiety of the Texas barbeque. She climbed into her sporty Corvette and jerked it into gear, whizzing past the silver and gray Cadillac. Her new life alone in Texas had begun! And she sped rapidly away from it, toward the solitude of her own run-down, depressing home, just down the road.

CHAPTER TWO

Kathryn slept restlessly. The unfamiliar sounds of the country—animals and frogs, even trucks on the nearby highway—kept her awake. Something else bothered her, too. *That man.* She couldn't get him out of her mind. Matt Logan. He was everything Emery wasn't—large and athletic, gregarious, people-loving. And yet, she was attracted to him. He had a magnetic charm that drew her to him, held his vision in her mind, reminded her of his touch.

As streaks of light entered her bedroom, she rose, pulled the long satiny robe tightly to her slim waist, and padded barefoot through the old house. Her classic clothes and poised carriage gave her an elegant appearance with deep burnished hair contrasting in the early morning shadows to her fair, Dresden-like complexion. Her sensitive brown eyes traveled around the dilapidated house while she waited for the water for her tea to boil. She seemed so out of place in this house that was once, as its very best, a farmhouse. But now, after years of being a widower's home and even more years of standing empty, the place was in sad disrepair. And Kathryn . . . lovely, refined

Kathryn, was being forced by life's circumstances to live here and try to carve a reasonable life out of this wreckage.

She gazed out the kitchen window where shafts of pink rays preceded the sun's rising. The age-old question, *Why me?* rose in her subconscious before she could push away the self-pitying thought. *I'm here and I'll make the best of it,* she resolved silently. But she didn't really believe it. Not on this particular morning. The house was too old and ugly, the customs here too strange, the men too bold.

The men. There had been another man besides Matt at the barbeque who made sure she remembered him. And this one was married! Oh—could she handle all this? Could she hold her meager life together while other forces tugged at her? But, she just had to; there was no one else now. She only wanted to devote herself to one thing at a time, starting with the house.

She assessed the rooms around her. There was so much work—hard work—to be done to make the place livable, she didn't know where to begin. Doors were warped, paint chipped or gone completely, floors bare—how in the world would she manage to do all that needed to be done? How would she afford it? Could she tolerate living here in the country, even if she made the place decent? After yesterday's experience at the barbeque, she wondered doubtfully. So far, the new life-style didn't seem to be suiting her.

The whistling of the teakettle attracted her attention and she turned all efforts and thoughts to preparing the cup of tea. Her worries, her life, were just too depressing. As she lifted the cup with a slender, well-kept hand, her rose-colored fingernails clicked against the expensive china, ringing ever so softly. Both Kathryn and the cup looked out of place in the run-down house in Texas.

She walked slowly through the house, sipping her hot tea, trying to put the necessary repairs into some kind of priority. After all, she was here and she had to tackle the job before her. And that job was monumental. It should keep her too busy to think of Emery—or Matt.

The kitchen was old, with limited cabinet space. The appliances were outdated and the oven didn't even work. The cabinets were wooden and had been painted numerous times. Perhaps the whole room should be gutted and new kitchen facilities installed.

The tiny adjoining breakfast room opened onto a large den, which covered the entire width of the house across the back. There was a single outside door, which Kathryn knew must be enlarged and replaced with a glass one. That would bring the lovely woods behind the house into full view. *Yes.* She smiled thoughtfully. *That would be very nice.* She opened the door and stepped outside. On bare feet, she walked through the dew-laden grass and decided this would be a great patio area with a brick floor arranged in a herringbone pattern. Her thoughts were broken by the distinct sound of a car approaching her house by way of the long driveway that led from the road.

A pang of fear gripped her momentarily as she heard the motor stop and the door slam. What should she do? Where could she run? Frantically she looked around for a weapon to protect herself. There was nothing close by. The sounds of an uneven gait reached her. In another moment, crutches and a man's blond hair were visible. Matt Logan!

His voice was hushed in the dewy quiet of the morning. "Kathryn, are you out here?"

Her heart pounded wildly and at one time she was both angry and relieved! "You . . . you scared me, you know," she accused, revealing her presence pressed close against the house.

He stopped and stared momentarily, the vision of her taking his breath. Her copper hair lay in unruly curls around her shoulders, her brown eyes were large and round with fright, the satiny robe was wrapped tightly around her bosom as she stepped into full view. He tried to keep his eyes on her face, but they deceived him and roamed her entire length, taking in her womanly beauty that was covered but certainly not hidden by the long robe. She possessed an aura, a certain presence of experienced self-awareness that was lacking in the younger women he knew. In essence, she was a special woman, and he knew it from the start.

He was immediatcly apologetic. "Kathryn, I'm sorry I scared you. I . . . saw your light from the road. I hope you don't mind my stopping by so early. I . . . Davis and I are going fishing."

Irritably she snapped, "Not at all. I always entertain men at six o'clock in the morning in my nightgown! What are you doing here?" She gestured, moving one graceful hand palm-up, trying not to appear nervous. Neither had been extremely gracious the last time they met.

Matt's appealingly tanned face masked his thoughts as he imagined how it would feel to have that enticing hand touching him. With a slightly sheepish grin, he admitted, "I want to apologize. I was rude to you yesterday and believe it or not, I'm not usually like that. I know now that I came on a little too strong, and I'm sorry if I offended you."

Kathryn dropped her arm to her side, her eyes meeting his sincere blue ones. She certainly hadn't expected this. "That's quite a speech, especially coming from you." Was her tone too acid? Why did she respond that way to him? Once again, she felt slightly flustered by this man.

"Is that your charming acceptance of my apology? I really want us to be friends, Kathryn, but not at the risk of losing my pride." His chin squared defensively.

36

She propped one fist on her hip. "And I'm supposed to be flattered?"

He leaned back on the crutches and his eyes narrowed slightly as he spoke levelly. "No. But it would be nice if you'd climb down off that high horse you're riding and give everybody a fighting chance. You might even enjoy it."

For a long moment, they stood in the dew-wet grass, appraising each other. Matt's words hit Kathryn hard, and suddenly she was seeing herself as others did. Perhaps she had been somewhat snobbish since her arrival. Certainly Matt saw her that way. And he had the audacity to tell her!

A million thoughts raced through Matt's head, including regret, as he tried to guess from her expression what in hell she was thinking.

Breaking the heavy silence, Kathryn blinked, and her eyes crinkled with laughter. "Maybe you're right, Matt. I've been a snob. And you know something? It's not much fun! I apologize, too. I was unnecessarily rude yesterday."

A smile of relief spread over his tanned cheeks, and he took a step toward her, holding out a large hand. "Friends, then?"

"Friends!" she agreed and laughingly shook his hand.

He held her hand for a moment. "I was so surprised to find such a classy dame as you at Dave's house that I just spouted the first thing that came into my head. I should have known better."

Kathryn cocked her head slightly to the side. Should she be truthful with this stranger, who, the previous night, had tried to seduce her? "To be perfectly honest, Matt, I've only been . . . single for a little over a year, and that was the first time I've been . . . ah . . . approached by a man. I think I handled it poorly, too."

He smiled, almost sympathetically. "First time? And

37

it's been over a year? My God, Kathryn, I find that hard to believe. You're a very beautiful woman. I'm surprised you don't have men falling at your feet!"

She blushed prettily, then laughed with embarrassment at her involuntary reactions. She pulled her hand gently from his, not really wanting to, but knowing she should. "Thank you, Matt. I guess I've lived a sheltered life until now. And you . . . you flatter me."

He shrugged and leaned uncomfortably on the crutches. "Just telling you the truth, ma'am. Just the truth."

She smiled, feeling suddenly at ease and found herself doing something that, last night, would have appalled her. "I'm having a cup of tea. Won't you join me for some, or would you rather have coffee?"

Surprisingly, he agreed. "Don't mind if I do. And tea will be fine."

"Come on in. I'll fix it, then we can sit out here if you like." She led the way to the kitchen and chatted amiably as she prepared a cup for him. "I've been trying to assess this old worn-out house, wondering if there's any hope for it."

While she spoke, Matt hobbled around the den, looking over the bare unkempt house, then on into the small living room. Kathryn followed him, waiting for the water to boil. "This place is in pretty bad shape, Kathryn," he agreed. "I guess I didn't realize it until now. From the road, it seems nice. Quaint, but nice enough."

"Now you see the truth. I didn't realize it until I arrived! It's worse than my wildest imagination. I figured it would be worn because it hasn't been lived in for so long. But Uncle John must not have done a thing to the place to keep it up after his wife died. And that was a good twenty years ago!" She sighed, unable to hide her disappointment in the house, or her deeper feelings. "So now I'm stuck here and don't really know where to start."

"Stuck here? Does that mean you can't leave?" He looked at her sharply and in a new light.

She nodded morosely, revealing to Matt what she had been reluctant to say aloud to anyone, even Hal. "I can't afford it. This place is paid for and . . ."

"And that's why you came here?" he finished, realizing that the attractive young widow who dressed impeccably and drove a flashy, expensive sports car was actually broke.

Instinctively, Kathryn's inner fight for self-preservation surfaced. She raised her chin. "I made every effort to sell this place. I tried not to come here, believe me. I sold everything else I own—except my car—everything! I paid the bills, cleared things with creditors and Uncle Sam. And this miserable hunk of junk of a house is what I'm left with!"

There was an uneasy silence. Kathryn's abhorrence to be where she was . . . doing what she was doing had finally surfaced—and she didn't know why. Why *now?* With this man?

In a weak attempt to assuage the strain in the small room, Matt chuckled and commented sarcastically, "I can see why it didn't sell. There isn't much of a market for a broken-down farmhouse in a small, static Texas town. Not unless you're looking for certain things." Then, his voice changed to a more serious tone. "But there are some benefits to be found here, you know. The people, the life-style . . . even the challenges. And this house, while I'll admit it does have problems, isn't hopeless."

"Challenges?" scoffed Kathryn. "I can't imagine challenges in this one-horse town!"

He raised one eyebrow and folded his arms defensively. "Well, sometimes challenges come built-in, like with this little mayor's race for me. All the challenge I can handle right now comes with the job. But sometimes you have to go out and create your own. Now, you may have to do a little digging, Kathryn. And I suspect you've had an easy life and never had to dig for anything before."

Indignantly, she ruffled. "How do you know what I've ever had to do?"

Before she could stop him, he had cradled one perfectly manicured hand in his coarse one, caressing her wrist with his other hand. His long fingers gently followed the faint trail of veins and lingered on her knuckles before tracing her fingers to the tips of her nails. "I know because these hands are so soft, and the nails so perfect. They are the hands of a pampered woman, Kathryn."

She gasped softly, angry at his offensive words, agitated by his touch. The warm, soothing contact with Matt's hands sent chills over her, and Kathryn fought for control. She couldn't believe her sensitive, girlish reactions to his closeness, his virility. After all, he was only a man, only . . . Matt Logan . . . *oh dear* . . .

She managed to sputter, "Pampered woman? Do you call what I've been through during this last year the easy life?"

"No," he admitted, looking down at her hand which he continued to caress.

"Then don't patronize me for what I am! I'm not to blame for this tangled mess! I'm only caught in it. And I can do whatever I have to do, believe me!"

His voice was low and sensuous. "I'm sure you can."

She was beginning to shake slightly. "Then, don't tell me what to do!"

"I wouldn't think of it, Kathryn. I believe you should be pampered. And, lovely lady, I'd like to do the pampering. I can do whatever it takes to make you happy, believe me," he murmured, smiling slightly and tugging on her fingers as he brought them to his velvet lips.

Kathryn was mesmerized for the moment, watching the

motion of his lips as they played on her skin, before she decided to jerk her hand away. But he held it firmly.

"I . . . I don't need anyone to pamper me! Especially you!" The words bounded uncontrolled from her astonished lips. "And I don't want you to think . . . well, just because I offered you a cup of tea, that I'm inviting you to . . . uh . . . I'm not looking for a man!"

The moment was punctuated by the shrill whistling of the teakettle.

"What are you offering, then?" he asked above the loud whine.

At that moment, she managed to free her hand. "Just that, Mr. Logan. A cup of tea. And that's all!" She whirled and reached for the kettle, which refused to hush until someone removed it from the gas flame. Kathryn bent her head to her task, but felt Matt's gaze burning the back of her neck as she worked. He was quiet for a few moments and she wondered what he was thinking. He probably hated her, laughed at her outburst. Then why didn't he just leave? That would solve everything and she could be rid of Matt Logan.

His slightly accented voice quelled her thoughts. "Ah, Kathryn, you don't have to worry about me. I never force myself where I'm not wanted. Somehow, I thought you invited me in here."

"It wasn't my idea for you to come at six in the morning," she sniped, handing him the steamy cup of amber tea. "I was just trying to climb down off my high horse, as you said, and be friendly."

He chuckled low in his chest and she noticed the blue shirt that matched the blue of his eyes. "You're right. I'll take the blame for this inconvenient hour. But some of the best encounters are spontaneous, and this visit definitely wasn't planned." He set the hot cup on the counter and

41

ambled, via the crutches, through the den. "Now, let's see what you have here."

Kathryn stared after him, still quivering inside from their close encounter, the suggestive comments. How could he now be so blasé . . . so nonchalant? It obviously hadn't affected him as it had her. This encounter was nothing compared with the dozens of glamorous women he'd undoubtedly had. He was just trying her out because she happened to be here at the moment. Well, he had her answer, so why didn't he just leave? She had been as concise as she could, under the circumstances. Reluctantly, she followed him into the small living room.

"I can see that you have your share of challenges right here in this house." Matt nodded his curly head toward the front door. "You might start with that warped door. The rain has really taken its toll over the years."

Her voice was without enthusiasm. "It's warped shut. I can't even open it."

"Well, it needs to be replaced," he decided as he perused the room. "Actually, except for the door, the room isn't too bad. A good cleaning and a coat of paint, something different at the windows and on these bare floors would fix this room up nicely."

Kathryn quirked her head at him. "Don't tell me— besides a professional football player and candidate for mayor, you're also an interior decorator!"

He laughed heartily. "My God, no! But I'm willing to do the work and help paint . . . if you pick out the colors and tell me what to do."

She stared at him for a moment. Tell him what to do? Why was he offering to help her? After their exchange, he knew where she stood. Before she had time to answer, Matt moved past her and stopped in the middle of the den floor.

"The fireplace seems to be in good shape. We just need

42

to clean it and make sure it draws. You'll be needing it soon. But this kitchen . . ."

Kathryn again tailed after him. "I was thinking of gutting the entire thing. I'd like a more modern kitchen." Why was she telling him this?

"Oh now, Kathryn, you don't want to do that. Kathryn . . . that's a mighty formal name for someone. Do you mind if I call you Kate . . . or Kaye? How about Kaye? That seems to suit you."

She stopped short and looked straight ahead, pondering the new proposal. No one had ever tried to change her or her name. But somehow, coming from Matt, it sounded right. Maybe Kaye suited her better . . . now. She looked at him, his blue eyes questioning and serious.

"Sure, why not?" She smiled at him and golden flecks lit her woeful eyes.

"You're very beautiful when you smile, Kaye. You should do it more often." His Texas drawl was low and husky.

She looked down modestly, dark lashes feathering her pink cheeks, and stirred her tea furiously.

When she was silent, he cleared his throat. "Now, as I was saying, these cabinets are all wood. You just don't find that often nowadays. They could be stripped of the paint, and maybe we could find a local cabinetmaker to construct more cabinets to match what's already here. Then we could get all the modern conveniences you want and . . ."

She looked at him curiously and questioned, "We? Don't you have enough to do?"

"Of course, I do. But you can use a little help around here and you know it. I'm offering . . . for free. You aren't refusing my offer, are you?" His expression told her he meant it. But free . . . ? There had to be a catch somewhere. She was wise enough to know that.

She shook her head and her chestnut hair moved softly. "No, I'm not refusing help, but I just don't see how—or when—you'll be able to work here. And why bother?"

"You're right. Until this election's over, my time will be limited. But there's only a little over a month to go and"—he shrugged, ignoring her question—"after that, I'll be free."

"You sound as though you don't expect to win. What if you became the next mayor?"

He looked at her curiously. "I have no illusions of that happening."

She smiled devilishly and turned to go back outside. "Well, good. Then you won't be too disappointed."

"Uh, Kaye? Kaye, would you mind . . . ?" His voice was a plea.

She whirled around, abashed that she had forgotten he was on crutches and had left him with a steaming cup of tea. "Sorry," she mumbled and relieved him of it, so he could hobble behind her to the backyard.

They settled into ancient weathered chairs and sipped the tea quietly for a while, gazing out into the pleasant woods that edged the deep backyard.

"I can see this area as a nice patio," Kathryn offered. "The floor should be bricks, laid in some interesting pattern, with a patio table and chairs over there and lights there and there . . ." Her enthusiasm grew as she imagined what the place would look like.

Matt joined in her fun. "And a big brick barbeque pit right over there!" He pointed to the perfect spot.

A sharp pang of painful remembrance hit her and immediately pictures of the days in Delaware when she and Emery had constructed their own barbeque pit conjured in her mind. Her brown eyes clouded briefly as she tried to mask her feelings. She looked away and murmured softly, "A barbeque pit would be fine . . ." But deep inside

44

Kaye wondered if anything in her life would ever be "fine" again.

"Kaye, what are you thinking?" Matt looked at her with concern, aware that he had touched a soft chord, just not sure what.

"Hmm . . . ? Just wondering why you're here now, and why you're planning to come back." She turned serious chestnut eyes to him. "I told you as clearly as I could that I'm not . . . available. It will do you no good."

He leaned toward her and his tone was equally serious. "I'm not sure why, Kaye. Maybe I believe I can teach you to love again. But I do know one thing—I'm glad you didn't sell this place. I would never have had the pleasure of knowing you. Or trying to."

Kaye smiled shyly, still unable to say that she, too, was glad. Softly she admitted, "Matt, I don't want to love again. It hurts too much when you lose."

He looked into her sweet, sad eyes. "Maybe I could change your mind. I'd like to think we could be friends, at least."

She shrugged. "Well, friends, maybe. As long as you know the odds . . ."

There was a spark of hope in his blue eyes as he smiled. "I always did like to gamble. I . . . I guess you and I are the only ones crazy enough to come to this one-horse town, Kaye."

Her deep brown eyes met his and an invisible, mystical bond between them was sealed. They were both searching, floundering, homeless. "Yes, I suppose so," she agreed quietly.

They talked for over an hour and, by the time Matt left, the friendship was conceived. But was there enough nourishment for it to grow? Kaye laughed as Matt departed in a frenzy, saying that Davis would be fit to be tied! He had

45

forgotten about the planned fishing trip. He was thinking of how to make his gamble a sure bet!

Kathryn . . . Kaye watched Matt's Cadillac streak out of her driveway, wondering why she had allowed this Texas stranger to enter her home, revealed her embarrassing financial status to him, and agreed for him to change her name . . . and her life. Was it the challenge that they had absolutely nothing in common, or because they shared a stronger bond?

Kaye spent the following week scrubbing and scrapping on the old house. It was a time for settling in—both physically, as she moved clothes and furniture to their proper niches, and mentally, as she assimilated into her new surroundings with a renewed, positive attitude. Part of the reason for her improved attitude was Matt Logan. Kaye reflected many times on their early morning talk . . . it had been a strange beginning for them. After that, she tackled the work before her with renewed vigor. Maybe there *were* some values worth working for in this small town, this worn house, these new friends. Maybe she could restore her own broken spirit as she rebuilt the old house. Maybe she would see Matt Logan again. Maybe not . . .

Kaye stopped comparing Delaware with Texas, her old life to her new, what-was with what-is. Her thoughts went from *What am I doing here?* to *Here I am, Texas!* Making the new life worthwhile became her goal, her challenge. It was just what she needed, to be busy, interested in something . . . or someone. And Matt Logan was becoming a part of her new life. Several times during the week, he stopped to check on her, to chat, to add a smile. And she was beginning to look forward to his visits, and to enjoy them.

Another new friend for Kaye was Nan Chandler, who came to help in the old house whenever she could. Although they were dissimilar in life-style and background, they liked sharing each other's company and friendship.

"Nan, I really appreciate all of your help. I could never have done all this without you." Kaye sat back on her heels and wiped her brow with the back of her grimy hand.

"Oh, sure you would. Maybe not as fast, though. I'm well known for my cleaning ability, so this is made for me!" Nan chuckled as she stood back from the window she'd been washing and checked it for streaks. She was wearing cut-off jeans and a huge football jersey that hid her hips.

"But this is above and beyond the call of friendship, you'll have to admit." Kaye stood and stretched. Her cuffed aqua shorts and matching pullover were stained beyond restoration, and a once-fashionable scarf hid her copper hair, protecting it from the flying dust they stirred up in the old house. "How about a cup of tea?"

"Make mine iced tea. I don't know how you can stand a hot drink on a day like this!"

"Iced tea it is, then," agreed Kaye.

Nan followed her into the kitchen and washed her hands before slumping onto a stool. "You know, I don't think old John Coleman ever washed a window in this place. Those back windows were horrible!"

"Well, look at it this way. Once they got the appropriate coating, he didn't have to worry about curtains!" Both women made faces and giggled like young girls. "Looks great now, Nan. It's so much lighter! Here you go . . . iced tea. Doesn't this place ever get cool? It's September!" Kaye slid Nan's glass of tea across the counter and sipped her own, accepting the Southern tradition of iced tea. Her hands were no longer delicate-looking. The nails were broken and chipped, the skin red and blotchy, the shiny polish speckled. They were the hands of a hard-working woman.

Nan eyed Kaye with a wry smile. "It should be cool by Christmas."

Kaye spread her damaged hands out before her. "It'll probably be Christmas before these hands will be the same, Nan."

"Oh, Kaye, when the house is completely renovated, you can let your nails grow again. And they'll be as lovely as ever." Nan smiled generously at her new friend.

Kaye sighed and shook her head. "I don't think I'll ever be the same as I was the day I drove into town. That was only a week ago! I've changed, my life-style has really changed . . . why, even my name is different!" She laughed, thinking of the Dresden-doll appearance she used to maintain.

Nan's tone was slightly chiding. "That crazy Matt! You shouldn't let him change your name . . . unless you want it, of course. I like Kathryn as a name."

Kaye shrugged. "Kaye is . . . shorter. It seems to suit me better—now anyway. Don't you think so?"

"To be honest, when I hear 'Kathryn Coleman,' I think of some stranger back in Delaware. But Kaye is right here in Texas."

"That's exactly what I mean. Kaye is here in Texas—to stay!"

"I'm glad to hear it, Kaye. I'd hate to think I was cleaning all these windows for somebody else! I'm dying to know what you think of Matt? Isn't he just fantastic?" There was something of a little-girl spirit in her question.

Kaye looked up quickly, too surprised to answer right away.

Instantly the little-girl quality was gone. "Oh, I'm sorry, Kaye. I shouldn't pry. It's just that I like Matt so much, and I guess I want you to like him, too."

"That's why you invited me to the barbeque at your

house, isn't it, Nan? Trying to be matchmaker?" Kaye chided gently.

"Oh, no! Well, maybe it looks that way, but—I hope you're not angry with me, Kaye," Nan said earnestly.

"Of course not. You and Davis are old friends of Matt's, aren't you?" Kaye ran a slender finger around the rim of her glass. She really didn't care to know about him. She was just curious.

Nan's curly brown hair bobbed enthusiastically. "For over ten years. He and Davis go back to pro-football days together."

Kaye raised her eyebrows. "Davis played professional football with Matt?"

"Yes." Nan giggled. "Can you believe it? My big lug was once starting linebacker for the Green Bay Packers. He just lasted two years in that north pole, but it was long enough to become good friends with Matt. The four of us—Matt was married at the time—clung together socially. Matt's from Dallas and you know how Texas boys stick together."

"Married?" That put a different light on things—or did it? Kaye really didn't care.

"It didn't last long. She and Matt were so different, I often wondered why he married her. Except that she was beautiful . . . and her father was rich."

"Good combination," Kaye admitted wryly.

"I think that her father and Matt have formed some businesses together since the divorce. They're still friends."

"He and his former wife?" Kaye's back stiffened. Just curious, of course. What did Matt's past life have to do with now?

"Oh, no! He and his former father-in-law are friends. I doubt that he ever sees Megan any more. They were only married about a year. After the divorce, Matt would visit us occasionally. He and Davis enjoyed fishing or sometimes he would help Davis with whatever job he was doing at the time. I remember one time they were branding the heifers. Matt was hysterical . . . almost got himself branded in the process of helping! But he still seemed to enjoy our country life-style."

"So that's why he came here to Twin Oaks when he retired from pro ball?" Kaye laughed at the mental image of Matt and Davis branding cattle.

Nan shook her head. "No, not really. He was very upset when the injury forced his early retirement, so Davis just invited him here for a while."

"I remember Matt's announcement on TV last spring. I never dreamed that I would meet him. Small world, isn't it?" Kaye said, grinning.

Nan instinctively placed her hand on Kaye's arm. "And you will be so good for him, Kaye."

Immediately Kaye stiffened at the inference. "I will?"

Nan responded quickly. "I mean when . . . if you. . . . if you could know him . . . Oh, Kaye, he's really a neat guy. That's what I mean."

"Nan," Kaye began gently, "I know you mean well, but don't bother. I've already told Matt. I'm not looking for a man."

"You have? You did? And, what did he say?"

Kaye laughed. "That he'd take his chances. He's coming to help paint the house this weekend!"

Nan was extremely relieved and laughed with her friend. "Oh, good. I think Davis is supposed to come over and help him with a door."

Kaye nodded. "My front door. Just out of curiosity, how did Matt get mixed up in small-town politics?"

"Oh, that!" Nan scoffed. "Well, he and Davis were sitting around one evening, enjoying a few beers and solving the problems of the world. By midnight, they were down to the problems of this county, laughing about the small-town politics. Unfortunately, Davis got serious. He was furious because Gil Ashland was running for mayor—for his fourth term—unopposed. That man has this little town in the palm of his hand. Davis just wanted someone —anyone—to present an opposing view. By the time they ran out of beer, Matt had laughed himself into being our mayoral candidate! The next day he couldn't believe what he'd agreed to!"

"Serves him right!" Kaye grinned at the mental picture of the two men settling the political future of the town over a few beers. "Mayor Ashland seems well liked, Nan. Everyone was extremely nice to him at your party."

"Oh, sure! Half those people there owe that man something. They don't dare speak out publicly. That's why we couldn't get anyone local to run against him. No one here would do it."

"Hmmm. Makes sense. And since Matt isn't a permanent resident . . ."

"Of course, Matt had to establish a residence here to qualify as a candidate, but he is just strong enough not to be influenced by the mayor's power. Now the people have a choice and, even though they may not say much publicly, no one will know what they do on the secret voting ballot. Wouldn't it be exciting if Matt won?"

"I don't know. He seems to be dragging his feet, Nan," Kaye answered truthfully.

"He's definitely the reluctant candidate," Nan agreed. "But Ashland is such a crook . . . oh, don't get me started on him now! He's one person you should stay away from, Kaye."

"Yes . . . I gathered that from our brief meeting the other evening." Kaye's intuition had been right. Even though Nan failed to be explicit, her hints were enough for Kaye to know he was dangerous. Changing the subject, she said, "I think we should call it a day, Nan. Don't you?"

Nan motioned with her curly head. "What are you going to do with that spare room full of old furniture? Do you want me to have Davis haul it off?"

Kaye looked thoughtful for a minute. "I don't know. Frankly, I haven't even looked in the room. I just closed the door and forgot about it. Why don't we take a quick peek now?"

Nan led the way. "Some of it may be useful, if you like old-fashioned furniture. Mrs. Coleman was an immaculate housekeeper, which probably explains why her husband couldn't do a thing around here after she was gone!" Laughing together, the two women began to prowl through the piles of chairs and tables, stacked floor to ceiling in rows so narrow they could barely squeeze between them.

"Nan! Here's an oak washstand! And the wooden dowels are still intact! And a draw-leaf table! And they're in mint condition!"

Nan gazed unconcerned in the direction of Kaye's excited voice. "Yes? Well, if you like them, they're all yours, kid."

"And Nan! A Hepplewhite chest! And a sideboard!" Kaye's voice rose with excitement at each find.

Nan picked up a mirror with an oval wooden frame. It had dark ebony wood and didn't appear special at all. "Do you really like these old things?"

Kaye's mahogany eyes gleamed. "Like? I *love* them! Nan, you don't seem to understand! These . . . this furniture . . . they are all antiques! Almost everything here is valuable! Very valuable!"

"Really?" Nan ran her hand along a dusty table.

"Oh, yes!" Kaye's enthusiasm was mounting by the minute. It was the most excited she had been in over a year. An idea, a marvelous, crazy notion was forming in her head. "Nan . . . do you know what I would just love to do?"

Nan looked at Kaye in amazement. "I haven't the slightest notion what you'll come up with next, Kaye!"

Kaye spoke slowly as her mind swirled. "I would love to open an antique shop! It's something I've always wanted to do. I just never had the chance . . . or the time. Now I have both . . . plus a great beginning of stock right here in my own house!"

Nan stared. "You want to open a shop here? In your home?"

"Oh, no. I want a larger shop, and in a good location, and something I can develop into a business people will drive over from Dallas for—it's not that far away . . ." Ideas were bouncing around her head at a dizzying pace.

Nan contributed to Kaye's ideas. "There's an empty shop on the square in town. Annie Malone's dress shop went out of business—and not a minute too soon! Talk about antiques! The place is still empty. It's a good location . . . on the corner of the square."

Kaye interrupted excitedly. "A corner shop on the square? Perfect! It sounds perfect! Oh, Nan! This could be just great for me. I really need something like this . . ." Her voice faded as she prowled happily around the musty furniture. "Wonder who owns the shop?"

Nan shrugged. "Don't know. But there's a big sign in the window with the phone number on it. And I'll bet there's an ad in the paper about it, too. It should be easy enough to find out."

"Great! Let's do it!"

They scrambled for the discarded morning newspaper and searched for the For Rent column. There were four items listed, and only one was a place of business.

"Spacious shop, corner, on square. That's it!" Nan read and pointed excitedly.

Then, the eyes of both women fell on the remainder of the advertisement: *G Ashland. 482–6000.*

"Oh, damn," muttered Kaye.

CHAPTER THREE

Kaye's eyes traveled above Gilbert Ashland's distinguished gray head where a handsome wood carving adorned the wall, next to a simple, primitive-style painting of a rural countryside. There were other items . . . his voice was mesmerizing, telling her about his constituents who had given these gifts out of gratitude. *For what?* She couldn't help wondering if they were really given or elicited as some sort of payment. *How unfair!* she thought suddenly. *He's done nothing to me to deserve that kind of judgment.* She snapped back to the impressive figure across the desk from her.

Gilbert leaned back in the walnut-toned leather chair. "I am always willing to help anyone who needs it, Kathryn. And I'm especially glad to be of help to you. Why don't we walk across the street and take a look at the rooms for rent. You can make sure it's what you want and need." His gray eyes smiled kindly at her and Kaye wondered if the things Nan had said about him were really true. He seemed so genuinely helpful.

"Yes. I'd like to do that," she agreed and rose to accompany him out of his office.

It was a short distance from the mayor's small but impressive offices, across the courthouse lawn, to the corner building. The typical Texas small-town square offered the perfect setting for the antique shop Kaye had in mind. The buildings were certainly dated, adding to the quaint old-fashioned location with the courthouse square, surrounded by a distinct row of shops and buildings on all sides. *Yes,* she thought, surveying the area silently, *it's just what I want.*

The keys rattled and the mayor unlocked the front door. Their footsteps echoed in the empty room as they stepped inside the spacious area. Because it was a corner shop, there were windows along one wall. Mentally, Kaye could picture a round mahogany table with a couple of Queen Anne chairs near it, offering a cozy, intimate feeling and coffee for her guests. She smiled and spoke for the first time. "Mayor Ashland, this is just perfect! I think it'll be fine."

"Now, wait until you've seen it all," he advised, taking her elbow and leading her to the rear of the building. "And, please, Kathryn. Call me Gil."

She laughed nervously. "Okay. If you'll call me Kaye."

He raised his eyebrows slightly, then nodded agreeably. "Kaye it is, then! Take a look at the back room. And the storage."

Kaye examined the spacious office area, which included a small bathroom, then a small storage area behind that. The room wouldn't serve to store much furniture, but she could use her own home for that. The main thing was the size of the showroom, and that was certainly adequate. After walking around the rooms again, Kaye turned a beaming face toward Gil Ashland. She couldn't hide her joy as she mentally visualized her business right here in this little brick store. She was thrilled with the prospect!

"I love it! I think it'll be perfect! Let's talk business. What are your terms?" Her eyes glowed as her enthusiasm mounted.

"Now, Kaye, don't jump at the first thing you find. You make sure it's what you want. Why don't you wait a few days . . . think it over. I'll hold it for you." His voice was kindly and his gray eyes fell gently on her, caressing her shoulders and appreciating her full bosom.

"Oh, there's no need for that, Gil. It's exactly what I want!" Kaye's enthusiasm was mounting each minute, as well as her curiosity about the terms. "Anyway, you know there isn't much choice in this town."

"Well, let's go back to my office and we'll work out something." He laid his hand gently on her shoulder and together they walked out of the empty building. They retraced their steps back across the courthouse lawn, but Gil dropped his arm from her shoulder by the time they were in public. His attentiveness was discreet. Or was it her vanity, assuming his admiration? Kaye wondered if she was just being too sensitive, or if there actually were subtle messages in his innuendos. She decided to give him the benefit of her doubts and assume he was simply being congenial.

Back in his office, Gil drew forth a few legal sheets. "The only request I'd like to make, Kaye, is that you keep your business here at least a year. And the monthly payment . . . no, that's too steep for a new business such as yours." He made a few notations on the paper, then handed it across the large mahogany desk to Kaye. "There, that ought to be satisfactory."

Kaye scanned the contract and protested when she saw the notation Gil had made. "Gil, I—this isn't enough rent. I just couldn't let you do that." He had crossed through the original sum and written the figure "one hundred" above it.

He leaned forward, his eyes intently on her. "Kaye, I know how hard this first year in business will be for you. The money isn't that important to me, anyway. Actually, I'm far more interested in keeping businesses in our town. I want the area around the square to be thriving and profitable for the people in this city."

"But this won't pay your taxes on the building, Gil. And I—"

"Nonsense, Kaye. You let me worry about the finances. I just want to look out my window here and see a bustling business in that corner shop . . . your business. It'll make me feel good to help you like this." He smiled warmly, and Kaye felt that he was sincere. How could she deny it?

"Well . . . I'm sure I could pay more rent . . . and I know I should . . . Oh, I don't know what to do . . ." Kaye shook her head, perplexed, but grateful for the tempting offer. She bent her head to read the contract fully.

"There is nothing to worry about, my dear," Gil laughed, trying to ease her doubts. "My mind's made up. I won't let you pay me more rent! And that's final!"

Kaye looked up from the paper and smiled. There was no doubt that she would find neither a more spacious store, nor a more suitable location for her business. And certainly not for one hundred dollars a month! It was too good to be true. Signing a year's lease seemed a small concession, and actually was in line with most renting procedures. She laid the papers on his desk and picked up a pen.

Gil interrupted her actions by placing his hand over hers. "Are you sure you don't want to wait a few days, Kaye? Think it over?"

Without a pause, she shook her head. "Your store is

perfect, Gil. And so is your offer. The sooner I sign, the sooner I can move in."

He smiled and lines crinkled around his gray eyes. "You're right, Kaye. You can start today."

As Kaye left Gil Ashland's office that day, she felt a strange combination of elation and apprehension, but she quickly shook it off. After all, there was work to do, and no time to worry about a decision already made. Kaye had a business to start and a place to put it. Humming a tune, she sped home in the blue Corvette. There was a future ahead for the first time in over a year, and Kaye rushed eagerly toward it.

A clattering racket accompanied the rumbling sounds of a car in the driveway, and Kaye peered curiously out the back door. "What's going on here?"

Immediately a dog began barking in the front seat of the silver and gray Cadillac. The warmth of recognition spread over Kaye when she saw the car. *Matt's here!* She hurried out to greet him, creating even more havoc—and racket—from the small, yelping ball of fluff in the vehicle.

"What in the world—?" she exclaimed as she waved a hand over the various paraphernalia piled on the plush suede and leather upholstery.

Matt's now-familiar face appeared from the open trunk where he had been bent over a stack of lumber and cans. The sight of her brought a smile to his tanned cheeks and, for a second, the car, the equipment, the noisy animal were forgotten as their eyes met. Then, the moment was gone and they continued to play their nice new-friendship roles.

"Hey lady, could you help a crippled guy with all this junk?"

Kaye approached him, hands on her slim hips, glaring from the man to the barking pup, back to the man.

Matt looked very casual and masculine in his cut-off

59

jeans and a short-sleeved gray pullover. The injured leg was stiffly wrapped in an Ace bandage, but there was a small box attached above the knee. He bent to unload paint cans and sundry equipment, leaning heavily on one crutch.

The entire scene was almost humorous and Kaye smothered her laughter as she demanded, "What are you doing? And what is that?" She pointed at his knee.

He ignored her questions and handed her a six-pack of beer. "Here. If I'm going to work around here, that hot tea just won't cut it. So I brought my own to drink."

Unthinkingly, she took the beer from him, their hands brushing briefly in the exchange. "If you're . . . what? Who said you were . . . ?"

He smiled and touched her nose as he hobbled past. "I did." He opened the car door and motioned to the yelping dog. "Come on, mutt. And shut up! That's no way to greet your new owner!" At his command, a golden woolly German shepherd pup bounded out, jumping first on Matt's legs, then at Kaye's.

She swatted absently at the dog and followed Matt. "What? New owner? Yours, of course!"

He turned to smile at her. "She's for you, Kaye. Isn't she cute?"

"Cute is not the issue, Matt. What do you mean, she's for me?"

"She is. I want you to have her. She's registered . . . a fine-quality animal. Look at that head . . . and the size of those paws!"

Kaye continued to follow him around the back of the house. "Matt, I've never had a dog. And, furthermore, I don't want . . ."

"But, Kaye," Matt interrupted, "you need her. She'll be a great watchdog for you. She'll protect you."

She spread her hands. "Protect me? I don't need a watchdog."

"The hell you don't!" Matt's sapphire eyes flashed at her. "Out here in the country, anyone could come here and you'd be helpless. No warning—nothing."

"I'm not helpless," she said quietly.

"No, but you are vulnerable out here. Do you remember the first morning I came?"

She nodded. How could she forget him with his intense blue eyes and his brazen manner. That was when he suggested that she shorten her name. Only a week ago . . . or was it two? She smiled, but he was dead serious.

"Kaye, anyone could drive up here just like I did. Anyone! Now, you'll be much safer with this dog to warn you. I'll feel better."

"Then what? So she warns me?" Kaye demanded.

He folded his arms and the muscles lay like weapons across his chest. "Well, you decide if it's someone you want around here. If not, you have this brave attack dog by your side and you give the command—*attack!*" His blue eyes twinkled merrily and a huge arm swooped around her. "Then you call me."

Kathryn laughed at his elaborate display and wriggled out of his arms. "I think I'll call you first!" She stooped to feel the fuzzy puppy that played at their feet. Setting aside the six-pack, she buried both hands in the downy hair. The golden pup looked up at her new mistress, immediately decided this was nice, and nuzzled closer. After a moment, Kaye looked at Matt. "I don't know the first thing about taking care of dogs. I've never had one."

He sat in one of the old chairs with his stiff knee extended. "Never? Not even a poodle? Somehow, I imagined you with a poodle . . . red ribbons on its ears and polish on its nails!" His voice was teasing, but his azure eyes were gentle.

She shook her head, one hand still caressing the grateful animal. "No. Emery didn't like—" she stopped abruptly. Why did she have to bring his name between them like that? *Why?*

"Not even a cat?"

"Nope. Nothing . . ." She didn't intend to say that, either. *Oh, damn!* She avoided Matt's eyes by watching the antics of the puppy. "She is cute and I like her, Matt."

"Well"—he broke the uncomfortable silence that followed—"she must be trained."

"To guard me?"

He chuckled. "No. That'll come naturally. She has to be housebroken, and, in a few months, we'll start obedience training so you can restrain her on command. She will be a very large animal in less than a year and you need to be able to control her."

Kaye nodded seriously. "What do I feed her? And where does she sleep?"

He laughed at her earnest naiveté. "Oh, you want to know the important stuff, huh? Well, we'll get to that later. And I'll help you with her, Kaye. I know big dogs can be a bother sometimes. But first, will you please do me a favor?"

She raised her eyebrows. "What?"

"Put my beer in the refrigerator before it gets too warm. I like it ice-cold!"

Kaye laughed with relief. This man was remarkable. He managed to put her at ease, even when she, herself, created the strain. She liked that. And she was liking him more every time she was around him. "By all means, let's take care of the really important things first!" Cheerfully, they entered the house together, accompanied by the mini-watchdog.

"Now, where should we start today? Hmmm, looks like

you've already started. The house looks—and smells—fresher already."

Kaye smiled. "Nan and I have been killing ourselves on this place all week. I'm glad someone can tell." She walked to the refrigerator with his package.

"I brought some basic off-white paint. I hope that's okay with you. Maybe we could go ahead with the painting today."

"That's fine. But first, satisfy my curiosity." She grimaced as she realized her suggestive statement.

Of course Matt picked up on it, devilment dancing in his eyes. "Oh, I'd be honored to satisfy anything, ma'am!"

Laughing, she pointed to his knee, where the tiny battery-sized box was strapped. "What is that thing on your leg?"

He propped his leg on a stool for the demonstration. "Glad you asked! That is a special transistor that turns me into the bionic man! Superhuman powers and all that! When I flip this switch, marvelous things happen. I can paint this room in ten minutes flat. Or I can turn into a love machine, but that takes considerably longer! Care to see how it works?"

"Matt! You're impossible!"

"Oh, I hope not. One flip of the switch—" He reached down and pushed it, pleased with the quiet humming noise it made. "That's just my motor getting started."

She folded her arms. "I'm waiting for the ten-minute painting job!"

He grinned appealingly. "Aren't you curious about the love machine?"

"No," she lied. "But I would like a truthful explanation of that . . . thing!"

He shrugged. "How disappointing. Actually, it's some damn transistor that sends little electrical shocks to these two muscles that converge above the knee. It's supposed

63

to help me utilize and exercise them better. It's part of my therapy."

"Electrical shocks? That's worse than the first explanation!" Kaye's face mirrored her amazement.

"See? You'd better believe the bionic man story! It's much more interesting!"

"Matt—"

"All right, Kaye. It's true. My doctor wants me to wear it several hours a day. The low-voltage electric current passes into the muscles and activates them. I can't seem to make them work, and this little gizmo stimulates the inactive muscles."

She looked at him skeptically. "Does it hurt?"

"Nope." He left the single crutch and headed out the door, limping.

She hurried after him. "Matt, are you sure you should be working around here? Is it too soon for you to be painting and hauling all that stuff? This can wait, you know."

"Believe me, Kaye, I'm fine. I need this exercise. The inactivity is getting to me. Don't forget, I'm usually a very active guy and painting is nothing compared to my normal fall schedule." He reached for an armload of paint cans and brushes.

She did the same and followed him back into the house. "How could I forget! Do you miss it?"

"You bet! In fact . . ."—he set the cans down on papers she had spread and turned to her, his blue eyes dancing— "my team is playing Miami this weekend, and I'm flying down to see the game. Would you like to go, too?"

"I don't think so, Matt. I have lots to do." Kaye was slightly aghast at his suggestion but tried to remain calm.

"Now, what do you have to do that won't wait? Come on, Kaye. It would be fun. I have to be back by Monday night. There is a debate at the high school with Hizhonor."

Kaye's eyes widened. *To spend the night?* She shook her head. "Thanks, anyway . . ."

"What's wrong? Don't you like football?" His tone told her it sounded preposterous.

"No, I mean, yes, I like it. It's just—" She stopped, realizing how inane she sounded.

He laughed and it rumbled deep in his chest. "Separate rooms. No demands, I promise!"

Instantly she blushed, feeling the warmth spread from her neck upward to her pink cheeks. *Damn!* she thought. *I'm reacting just like a schoolgirl! What's wrong with me?* She bent her head away from his penetrating gaze as she tried to open the paint can. His large, sure hands seized the chore from her shaky grasp and easily popped the lid. She looked up into his sturdy face, the jutting jaw so prominent and close. She could see a muscle jerking near his ear before he spoke.

"Well, at least come to the debate with me Monday night."

She took a shaky breath and suddenly her mouth was dry. She licked her lips before answering. "In all honesty, Matt, a political rally is not the way I want to spend my evening."

In a low voice he reciprocated. "In all honesty, neither do I."

"I'll let you know," she hedged and dipped her brush in the creamy paint.

Later, as they completed the finishing touches on the room, Kaye stood back to admire their work. "It looks great, Matt!"

He groaned and stretched before joining her, his arm resting casually on her shoulder. "I agree. Let's have a beer."

65

She tried to be nonchalant about his touch as she slipped away from his arm. "Sounds good. Come on. I have something to discuss with you. And to show you." The smug expression on her face piqued his curiosity and he followed her to the kitchen.

They gulped the beer and nibbled on crackers and cheese before she finally told him about her business. Kaye's brown eyes glistened with anticipation as she announced, "I'm going to open a business in town! My own business! An antique furniture shop!" She giggled like a schoolgirl, but Matt just stared uncertainly at her.

"A what?"

"An antique shop. Here, let me show you," she said, eagerly leading the way to the spare room that housed the antiques. Proudly she pushed the door open and allowed Matt to enter first.

"You can sell this old stuff?" he asked incredulously, walking slowly through the narrow aisles.

"You bet I can! This 'old stuff' is very valuable to some people. And very beautiful. It's all solid wood. You'll see when I get my shop set up." She smiled and her Dresden face fairly glowed as she talked.

Matt turned his attention to her. "Where are you thinking of having your shop, Kaye?"

"I've rented it already! And it's perfect! It's on the square, across from the courthouse, in a corner spot. It's going to be great."

Admiration lit his face. "You know, you're something else, Kaye. Not only are you beautiful, you have a smart head on your shoulders. I like that."

Modestly she smiled up at him, acknowledging his praise. It felt very good to please him. "Thank you, Matt. But, I must admit, I haven't always been so independent. Necessity is a great motivation. I was a very dependent

66

wife. Emery made all the major decisions for us. And they always seemed right."

"That's quite a legacy, Kaye. But no one is always right. Surely . . ." He paused and moved closer to her, sensing an uneasiness pulsate through Kaye.

She looked down, then back to meet his blue eyes levelly. "Well no, as a matter of fact, he wasn't always. He made a few blunders in investments and . . . planning."

Matt's voice was husky. "Hey, I didn't mean to . . . Mistakes are human, Kaye. We all make them. Just remember that, as you go along. Every decision you make on your own won't be perfectly right. But it'll be your decision. And that's even more important. I'm glad you'll have a job, a business, to keep you busy."

She smiled wanly. "Doesn't leave me much time to wallow in my sorrow, does it?"

"Now, Kaye. That's not what I meant."

She raised her head defiantly. "Did you happen to think that this is something I want to do? I've always wanted to have a shop of my own. I love antiques. And here they are. It's made for me."

He gazed at her for a long moment as she defended her actions.

"I'm delighted for you, Kaye. I'm glad you are now able to do something you've always wanted to do. It's a shame you waited so long." His tone was perceptive but gentle.

Kaye looked down. "Yes, I suppose it is, Matt," she murmured.

He cupped her chin with his big hand and tilted her face toward him. "Enough sermons for the day. Let's finish our beer and clean up the paintbrushes before they get stiff. I'd like to see this shop you've rented."

She smiled and nodded. "I'd like that."

She turned and together they walked back through the house, his arm resting on her shoulder, hers lightly around his waist. It was a warm, secure feeling to have him close, to laugh and work with him, to spend a day with Matt. Kaye had forgotten how nice it was to share. *Matt Logan —what are you doing to me?*

"Are you ready to go?" She stepped outside where Matt was cleaning the brushes. The pup romped nearby, chasing leaves.

"Almost. This stiff knee slows down my normal speedy efficiency." He leaned awkwardly over his task.

"What happened to the bionic man? Someone must have flipped your switch!" she teased, her laughter showering them lightly.

"Actually, ma'am, I'm saving it for later, more important work!"

"Well, you did some very important and beautiful work this morning, Matt. The room is fantastic. I really appreciate your painting it for me." She meant it seriously.

"It was a joint effort, remember?"

"Yeah, but you did most of the work, remember? Painting was never my forte."

He smiled at her. "I enjoyed it, Kaye. With this crippled leg, I'm not able to do much these days. This gave me a sense of accomplishment. There's something about paint on a wall that does that. I'm quoting from some famous philosopher, of course. Like Descartes or Plato."

"How about Michelangelo?" she said with a giggle. "Why do I feel like I'm doing you a favor because I let you paint my house?"

He paused and looked into her expressive eyes, grateful for the brief merriment he saw there. "Because you are. I had to think up some excuse to spend the day with you, didn't I?" He shook the brushes and took them to the garage for storage.

Kaye watched his receding back, wondering why. *Why is he here? Am I giving him an unspoken invitation? I don't*

*intend to . . . want to. Or do I? Oh, God—why? Not now.
Not this soon!*

When he returned, her eyes were round and large, with tears very near the surface. What happened to the happiness he observed only moments ago? Was it that fleeting?

Quickly she turned away. "How about another beer?"

"Sure," he agreed, reaching for the paint cans while she disappeared into the house.

Within minutes, they were relaxing in the ancient wooden chairs, chatting about where the patio would be. There was a lot of work ahead and he only hoped that he could be a part of it.

"Opening this business must mean you're planning to stay in Texas, Kaye. I'll admit, when I first met you, I didn't think you'd last long here."

She smiled and admitted, "Neither did I. But now, I have something to work for and . . . I guess it's a pretty good place to settle down."

He shrugged his huge shoulders. "It's not a bad place to be . . . close to Dallas, not too far from Houston. I like the people, of course, and the slower pace here. However, I know it's not as vibrant as the East and Delaware."

She sipped the beer slowly. "No, but I had to leave Delaware. Too many memories."

"I can understand that." They were quiet for a moment, each lost in thought. Then, after a long gulp of the frosty beer, Matt asked, "So, when are you going to show me your new store?"

Kaye shrugged, but there was an eagerness about her voice. "Whenever you're ready. It's in great condition. Doesn't need painting or anything. And I'll just need a few items of equipment—a phone and cash register. There is a large desk here that I can use and Gil says I can start moving in any time. I figure it'll take me about two weeks to get organized and ready for business."

69

"Gil?" Instantly Matt was on edge.

She nodded, unaware of his tension. "Ashland. I rented it from Gil. He took me through and it's perfect—"

A guttural, almost growling sound interrupted her as Matt exploded, "You rented your shop from Gilbert Ashland? Kaye! Of all the dumb, dangerous things to do, that's the worst! You don't know what a jackass he is! He's a crook—and you're placing the future of your business in his hands!" His face was livid with anger.

Instantly Kaye was on her feet to match his fury. "I had no alternative, Matt! His is the only shop available and the location is excellent!"

Matt stood, towering over her. "The only thing that's perfect is that he has you where he wants you!" His eyes were hard, and he held out his hand, the palm making a large cup.

Kaye propped her fists on her hips and glared at him. "He does not! All I did was rent from him!"

"Kaye, he can't be trusted. Don't you understand?"

"I understand that he's been very nice to me. The rent is extremely cheap, and the shop is perfect for what I need."

"I'm telling you the man can't be trusted. He's devious! I'll bet he couldn't wait to rent to you."

She shook her head. "He didn't pressure me at all, Matt. In fact, he tried to get me to wait and think it over before I signed."

His eyes narrowed. "You signed something? Oh, damn, Kaye! Why didn't you wait and talk it over with me? What did you sign?"

"It's just a year's lease. And why should I talk it over with you? My decision, remember?" She gestured toward herself with those delicate but durable hands.

"I could have helped you. I hope you won't regret signing that lease."

70

"You would have tried to dissuade me from signing. But you have absolutely no influence in my business affairs ... or any others, for that matter!" Her nostrils flared in anger as she slung her cutting words at him.

Matt shifted, as if he'd been struck. His tone was lower as he answered, sighing, "You're right, Kaye. I have no influence on you. But I do care what happens and I don't want you to get hurt. I know Gilbert Ashland, and he has other motives, believe me."

But Kaye would not be restrained. "Have you forgotten that I am the one who went to Gil about the shop? It was all my idea."

He shifted again, annoyed with her attitude, her biting words, her familiarity with his enemy. "What's all this 'Gil' stuff?"

Kaye's voice rose. "What business is it of yours? How dare you grill me like this? Just who do you think you are, Matt Logan?" Kaye trembled with the impact of her own words.

Matt recoiled with a sinking feeling inside, realizing he had pushed her too far and probably ruined everything he had worked to build between them. His voice was husky and spiritless. "You're right, Kaye. There is no reason for me to question your decisions or your actions ... except that I ... care for you. And, frankly, I don't know why in hell I do!"

He turned to go and, instinctively, Kaye reached for him. Her icy hands clutched his sinewy arm, trying to cling to him, to their eroding relationship. She couldn't let him leave like this. She just couldn't! "Matt, I ... I'm sorry. I didn't mean to ... I just ..." Kaye floundered, searching for the right words. She raised her deep mahogany eyes to him, and they expressed more than she could ever explain. The sadness, the confusion, the fear ... all were reflected there.

He reached for her. "I'm sorry, too. I shouldn't have pushed you . . ." His arms went around her and his eyes rested on her sweet, sensuous lips. "I know I have no right to interfere. I just . . . can't help myself . . ." And he kissed her waiting lips ever so gently, lingering like a velvet whisper on her yearning, sensitive soul. A soothing melody rose within her, and Kaye soared with the sweet song of beauty and passion. Yielding to the curve of his strong arms, the solid fortress of his chest, the solace of his healing kiss, she surrendered to the symphony of her desire. This was where she belonged—where she'd wanted to be all along—in his arms . . . knowing his passion . . . responding to his kiss . . . *Oh, God, no! How could I?*

Kaye gasped audibly with the reality of her position and pushed against Matt's inflexible chest. She had to get away from his arms. What was she doing? She was ashamed of her own heart-pounding reaction to his touch. "No! Please, don't—" Tears filled her eyes as she stared at him with alarm.

"Kaye, honey, it's all right . . ." He tried to hold her, his hands caressing her trembling shoulders.

"No!" she repeated frantically. "I hardly know you! And I don't want . . . I can't . . . oh, please . . ."

"Kaye?" He shook her gently. "Why?"

She just shook her head wildly. "It's too soon, Matt. Don't you understand? It's just . . . too soon," she finished in a whisper.

He grasped her shoulders with large, powerful hands, not allowing her to wriggle free this time. "I'm afraid I do understand, Kaye. I'm competing with an absolutely perfect memory! And it's damned impossible! Darling, you're living a lie. Nobody is—*was*—that perfect. Please don't wait too long, until you're bitter and hard. I'm not giving up on you. There's a lot of love beneath that steel armor you wear, and I intend to uncover it!"

"I think you're talking about lust, not love!" she spat at him, angry that she couldn't tear away from those penetrating blue eyes.

He pulled her closer so that his warm breath boldly brushed her face. "I'm talking about desire, armored lady! Don't tell me you've forgotten what that is! Or maybe you never knew!"

Kaye struggled to raise her impotent fist against him, but Matt moved with amazing agility. His sinewy arm wrapped around her, pinning one arm to the side as he jerked her against the hard length of his body. His other hand grabbed her wrist sharply as she flailed at him.

"How dare you—" she uttered contemptuously before he silenced her with his crushing lips.

The intensity, the power of his kiss took her by surprise, and Kaye opened her mouth for the instinctive cry of protest that bounded from her throat. She was humiliated when the sound came forth as a sensuous, guttural rasp. Matt responded by encircling her with both arms, pressing the muscled hardness of his thighs against her, revealing the virile strength of his desire. Immediately, his probing tongue invaded her inviting mouth, all-consuming and adamant. Ruthlessly, he controlled her entire being, demanding the response from her that he wanted . . . needed.

Her fist was free to pummel his shoulder, but at some point, Kaye became intoxicated with the dizzying thirst of desire. *When did it change?* The assault evolved into a gentle throb as Matt's lips moved to tingle the corner of her mouth, then blaze a trail to the sensitive hollow of her throat. A low, soft sound let him know she shared his need as she clung drunkenly to his arm, begging for more of his sweet, heady wine.

"Oh, Matt . . . ," she choked. The murmur of her own thick voice sobered her, filling her with realization and grief. Abruptly tears burned her eyes as she remembered

73

that her beloved husband was dead, and now she was in the arms of another man! A flood of pain overwhelmed her, and without warning, Kaye cried as she hadn't cried since the day of the funeral. She covered her face with delicate but weathered hands and sobbed. She was barely aware of the strong arms that enfolded her, the durable chest that cushioned her, the man determined to heal her wounds.

They stood clinging together for a long, long time. Kaye allowed the tears to flow, knowing there was no way to stop them. Matt accepted her grief, knowing there was nothing he could do for her except to hold her. And that is exactly what he did. No words were wanted or given. But a silent message of tender concern, perhaps of love, was transmitted from his strength, fortifying her weakness.

Finally, Kaye stopped sobbing, but continued to cling silently to the warmth and security of the man who held her. In time, her own time, she raised her head from his tearstained shirt.

"I'm . . . I'm sorry, Matt. I don't know what happened to me. I didn't intend to do that." Her voice was hoarse.

His hand, now gentle, caressed her face. "Don't apologize, Kaye. I understand."

She smiled wanly. "Thank you for being my shoulder to cry on."

He looked into her sorrowful brown eyes. "Do you understand that I want to be here? Let me help you, Kaye."

"Just hold me, Matt. Just hold me," she whispered.

So, he just held her, giving the comfort she couldn't possibly receive alone.

CHAPTER FOUR

Matt leaned toward her, his elbows on the table. "Are you sure you won't go to Miami with me? We'll stay at the beautiful Fountainebleau, swim in fresh or saltwater pools, go frolicking in the mighty Atlantic. I would take you to Wolfie's for the best hot pastrami and cheesecake south of New York. Then, we'll dine and dance in the rooftop restaurant of the Doral on the Beach, overlooking the city lights. It's just your style, Kaye . . . elegant, with silver candelabra and lace tablecloths. What do you say?" His sapphire eyes were aglow.

Kaye laughed warmly at his enthusiasm. "Does the Miami Chamber of Commerce pay you well for these spontaneous advertisements?"

"No, but do you think I have a chance with them . . . or with you? I also do a nifty soft-shoe—when my knee isn't in its present condition, of course. Come on, Kaye. Say you'll go with me. It won't cost you a dime. And"— his voice lowered as he continued—"and, no demands, I promise. Separate rooms . . . I won't embarrass you."

Kaye looked away from those convincing blue eyes of

his and took a deep breath. Matt was impossible . . . and very persuasive. Oh, she was tempted, with his promises. It sounded like fun. But, she didn't dare! She might be even more tempted under Miami's moon . . . enough to relent to her inner desires. She shook her head.

His large hand covered hers. "What can I say to persuade you, Kaye? Look, all I want is to take you someplace nice. We'll see a professional football game and enjoy a few of the sights of a beautiful city." He shrugged. "To be honest, I also want to show you off to my old friends. Does this embarrass you?"

Kaye looked into his eyes and, at that moment, wondered why she was refusing. He was making concessions for her, and she knew it. But why? Why was he even bothering with a stick-in-the-mud like her? "You're not embarrassing me, Matt. We've discussed this before, remember? It sounds wonderful to go to Miami with you, and I appreciate the offer. But I . . . a trip like that . . . it's just not . . ." She halted, thinking she was probably crazy.

"I know," Matt finished for her with a resigned sigh. "It's not your style." He struggled clumsily to his feet and, with the first step, nearly tripped over the new pup who frisked anxiously around their feet.

Kaye scooped the wriggling animal up in her arms, scolding playfully. "Curb your enthusiasm, dog. This man's not too steady on his feet yet. And we wouldn't want to be responsible for the other knee!"

Although Matt stung inside at her rejection to accompany him, he wouldn't reveal his disappointment. It was all a part of the game . . . her game . . . and she had warned him. His hand reached out to scratch the puppy's head. "What are you going to name her, Kaye?"

"Oh, I don't know. How about Fluffy? She's so cute and cuddly."

76

"Well, she won't be fluffy and cuddly forever. And she deserves a good German name like *Fräulein* or *Schatzi* or *Heidi*. Fluffy will sound strange when she lopes to meet you a year from now and she's half as big as you are!"

"How about Heidi? I like that! We'll name her after the lonely little girl who went to live with her grandfather on the mountain."

Matt's hand graced Kaye's cheek. "Like the pretty but lonely lady who came to live in Texas. Sounds appropriate. But wasn't it the grandfather who was lonely?"

Kaye shrugged and gazed nervously into the blue eyes that seemed ever closer. "Oh, I don't remember the story. But I'm not lonely any longer, with Heidi and . . . you, Matt."

His lips were very close and she could feel his breathing lightly on her face. "Me, either . . ." And he kissed her ever so gently, lingering while his indolent tongue traced her lips, pressing his chest against the pup that lay in her arms between them. Heidi wriggled uncomfortably, almost jumping out of Kaye's arms and rudely interrupting the intimate moment. "There's no chance of you changing your mind about coming to Miami with me?" Matt murmured.

Kaye smiled. "Afraid not. I have a responsibility, thanks to you. How do you like your new name, Heidi?" As if in answer, the eager pup looked up and licked Kaye's chin. "Aaugh! Dog germs!" Kaye screeched, laughingly dumping the frisky animal. She grabbed a tissue and began scrubbing vigorously at the tainted area.

"Hey, Heidi! Watch it! You're offending the lady!" Matt howled with laughter. "Oh, Kaye, are you in for a real learning experience with this little pup!"

"Hmmm. I can tell I am! But the burning question is, will she protect me?"

Matt kissed her nose. "Give this guard dog six months,

and I'll have to bribe her with dog biscuits in order to get close to you. In fact, I already have a year's supply of Doggie Crunchies! You know, we can always convince Nan to dog-sit while we're gone. I'm sure she wouldn't mind." He paused, but the apologetic expression in her eyes gave him the inevitable answer. He turned toward the door. "Well, if I can't interest you in a trip to Miami, can I expect you to attend a dull political rally in the school auditorium on Monday night? It's an opportunity to see your favorite politicians in action. Both Gil and I will debate."

After renting from Gil, Kaye supposed she should stay as neutral as possible in the political affairs of the two men.

"Matt, I don't really want to get involved in local politics. I hope you understand." With chagrin, Kaye realized that this was the second rejection of the evening.

"I didn't want to get involved either, but I'm into it now. What infuriates me is that a crook is running this small town. And my goal is to do something about it."

She looked at Matt doubtfully. "Can you prove he's a crook?" Kaye hated to think that she was renting from a dishonest man.

"No, I can't prove a thing because nobody in this whole, goddamn town will testify against him! We'd never have a chance in court! The only solution is to vote him out of office!" Matt's voice reached an alarming pitch and aroused Heidi, who began barking wildly.

"Easy, girl," Kaye soothed, a trace of teasing in her voice. "That's just our illustrious prospective mayor trying out his oratory skills!"

Matt glared at her disgustedly, trying for all his worth to portray a serious image. "All right! Make fun of me all you want, Kaye! But you already have an alliance with the man, and if you think you won't be affected by him, you're wrong. Actually, I thought you'd help me by taking this endeavor seriously . . . give me encouragement . . . accompany me to the debates . . ."

"Is that why you painted my room? And spent the entire day with me? And brought me this marvelous little pup? My, my, what you won't do for a vote!"

"I don't want your vote, dammit, woman! I want—"

But Kaye interrupted quickly. "I know what you want. We've already discussed that. I'll promise you one thing. You have my vote, Mr. Candidate." Her easy smile was interrupted by his kiss. This time, there was no pup between them—nor tears. And she responded to the pressure of his lips against hers, his tongue teasing her lips open, the breathtaking plundering of her mouth. She clung to his powerful shoulders, feeling the tenseness of his muscles poised so near to her, yet refraining. As she swayed against him, his rock-hard thighs supported her unfeigned willingness. In a moment of impassioned fervor, her own tongue reached out to meet his, blazing the intensity of his male desire for her. Soft, animallike noises escaped her throat, and she pushed herself away, reluctantly, albeit positively. "Matt, please don't. I'm hopeless," she whispered.

He nibbled at her sensitive earlobe. "And I'm a hopeless romantic. Everyone seeks love, Kaye. Even an armored lady. I'm not giving up on you, Kaye. You're too special."

"Matt, please . . ." She pushed against his muscular chest. "Have a nice trip to Miami. And let me know how the political rally goes. I'm sure you'll do fine without me."

"I don't know how fine, my pretty lady, but it looks like I'll have to do without you . . . for now, anyway." And he was gone into the night, leaving Kaye to wrestle with the regret that plagued her confused mind all weekend.

Although she was reluctant to admit it, Kaye was miserable the entire time Matt was gone. She blamed it on the weather. An early winter storm blew into Texas, leaving them 3.4 inches of cold rain in two days. That added to the remorse of missing out on a weekend in sunny Florida. She spent the days cleaning the chilly, empty shop until her fingers ached from the unaccustomed scrubbing and cold. Worse yet, Matt didn't bother to call. She hadn't heard from him in three days. But then, why should she? After she had rejected him so completely, Kaye couldn't blame him if he never contacted her again. But she knew she would regret losing him. *Losing him?* What was she thinking? How could she lose someone she never had? Not really, anyway. They were just friends. Considering the fact that they were "just friends," he certainly occupied a preponderance of her thoughts!

By Monday evening, the rain had stopped. *Oh good,* thought Kaye. *Maybe they'll have a good turnout at the debate. But why should I care? It's not my concern.* In the back of her mind, she knew that Matt was her concern. She just couldn't help it.

Kaye wandered into the kitchen of the dark, lonely house and wearily fixed herself a cup of spiced tea. She pondered about the status of the antique shop. The cleaning had been done, which explained her present state of near-exhaustion. Now, there would be a delay in her opening until she could apply for and receive her sales tax license from the state comptroller's office. That could take weeks, the way governmental wheels turned.

Kaye leaned on the counter and absently edged the cup with her work-roughened, scratchy finger. There was a time when her fingers were as satiny and lovely as her china, her nails as polished as the exquisite flowers on the hand-painted design on her imported Irish porcelain. She had always taken pride in her appearance, in the smooth touch of her hands, the elegance of her long nails. So had Emery.

Suddenly, tears welled up in her eyes as she felt her old emotions creeping in. Quickly, she wiped them away and picked up her cup. She grabbed a book and settled comfortably in front of the small fire that crackled merrily in the fireplace. Her eyes rested on Heidi, who lay sleeping peacefully in front of the fire, exhausted after a full day of chasing cobwebs and dust particles with her mistress. Kaye smiled involuntarily, grateful to Matt for contributing the small pup to her lonely life. It was impossible not to love her. She had already brought joy and humor with her. But Kaye supposed Matt knew that would happen.

Matt Logan . . . His handsome, athletic form loomed in Kaye's mind, and she wondered how the debate was going. Her lips curled into a smile and she touched them, recalling his kiss . . . gentle, fervent, passionate . . . frightening. Yes, frightening. Kaye had responded to him like a young schoolgirl. Scared! That was the word he had used. He had known her feelings right away, even though she denied them to herself as well as to him. And he was right! His kiss . . . his touch . . . had scared the hell out of her! How could he have known that? Did he also know her inner passionate response to his arousing kisses? Did he know that, even though he was totally different from Emery, he had awakened a longing deep within her that Kaye couldn't avoid. Did he also know she was fighting these feelings? That she was filled with guilt? Kaye was determined to avoid another relationship where she might get hurt . . . might give her love, only to have it ripped from her life, as it had been when Emery died. She wouldn't permit that kind of personal pain to paralyze her again. She didn't think she could bear it.

He would be in the midst of the big debate about now . . . *He?* Why was she thinking of *him?* What difference did it make in her life what Matt Logan was doing

. . . what *he* thought of her . . . what she said to *him*. Why was she spending so much time thinking of *him?*

Kaye opened her book and stared at the blurred lines of words. Somehow, she couldn't chase the massive male figure of Matt Logan from her memory. He was the most . . . the most masculine man she had been near in a long time. Well, *that* was it! She was physically attracted to him. It was her own lust that plagued her right now. *Oh, no! I can't do this to myself . . . to Emery's memory.*

A sudden, alert movement of Heidi drew Kaye's attention. The dog had been sleeping quietly, but something— or someone—had disturbed her. With sharp ears perked forward to catch every sound, she crept stealthily to the back door and poked her nose at the crack.

Kaye sat frozen, her imagination racing wildly as she watched her mini-guard dog in action. Abruptly, the sound of Heidi's shrill barking coincided with a loud, forceful knock on the door.

Above the clatter, Matt's voice boomed, "Kaye! Kaye, are you home? It's me!"

Relief flooded her being as she realized that the person on the other side of the door was, indeed, Matt. She padded quickly to the door, opening it to admit the man who had occupied her thoughts all evening—all weekend.

The dark doorway was filled momentarily with Matt's looming figure as he braced a huge arm on either side of the door frame. On his face was an expression Kaye had never seen. Anger? Frustration? Disillusionment? He stared at her for a long, breathtaking moment before rasping, "Damn! You look good to me, lady!"

"You . . . you appear at the strangest times, Matt. Are you all right?" Her mahogany eyes were wide with the anticipation of seeing him again.

He made no attempt to move or to answer her question. He just stood gaping at her, taking in her beauty. Kaye was clad only in the thin satiny robe and she shivered as she met his gaze. Finally, he spoke. "I hope I didn't scare you, Kaye. But I . . . I just wanted to see you. I have to talk to someone. Do you mind if I come in?"

She smiled invitingly at this hulking man who was asking for permission to enter her home . . . perhaps her life. He needed someone tonight. Well, so did she. "Are you going to stand there all night? Please come in where it's warm. Can I get you something?"

He limped past her, his huge shadow completely covering her momentarily. She inhaled his leathery fragrance and knew she wanted him near her tonight. Suddenly she had a wild desire to wrap her arms around him, comfort him, love him. She quelled the impulse, however, and allowed him to move past her without a touch. He went directly to her refrigerator and extracted one of the beers he had left there.

"Ah, Kaye, this is nice," he said with relish as he swigged the beer.

"How was your trip?"

He shrugged. "Fine."

"You're tanned. Was the weather nice?" She stood with her back to the fire, absorbing the warmth.

He nodded. "I spent Saturday on the beach. Weather was perfect. Hot, in fact."

"We had rain."

"And it's colder."

She nodded, wondering why they were suddenly so tongue-tied that all they could talk about was the weather. "Have a seat, Matt." She gestured toward the sofa.

He slumped down and leaned his head back to take in another gulp of the beer. Quietly Kaye refilled her teacup and sat on the opposite corner of the sofa, tucking her feet gracefully under her. Matt studied the flames, obviously preoccupied.

Finally, Kaye broke the silence. "Did you have a good crowd at the debate tonight? How did it go?"

He turned his face toward her and laughed wryly. "I thought you'd never ask!" His fixed smile remained as he shook his head from side to side. After another long swallow of beer, he continued. "It was awful. *I* was terrible! Even Davis was embarrassed!"

"Why, Matt? What happened?"

"I didn't do my homework on this job. It's as simple as that. I think you said it the first time we met. I thought I could come in here to this one-horse town and easily win this mayor's race because the public recognized my name. But I misjudged Gilbert Ashland. He's very bright . . . and shrewd. He tore me apart . . . in front of the entire town. And I had no defense."

"Oh, Matt, I'm sorry—"

But his voice was harsh. "Why are you sorry? Because I was so stupid? Oh, no, Kaye, it was my own fault. You were right. And so was Davis. I fixed my own wagon!" Matt stood and paced the floor, disturbing the quietly sleeping Heidi.

Kaye's tone matched that of Matt. "Okay, so you made a fool of yourself! Or you let Gil do it! At least you're admitting what happened . . . and who's at fault."

Matt stood and began pacing. "Oh, hell yes! I know. And if I didn't, Davis would damn-sure inform me! He's furious! And I don't blame him!" Matt's arms waved angrily in the air. "In fact, he wants me to quit! He thinks I'm already through—that I should just drop out of the campaign now, before I embarrass myself—or him—anymore!"

When he hushed, Kaye responded quietly, "Well, why don't you? It's what you want, isn't it? Here's your chance."

Matt stopped pacing and stared at her. A strange expression spread across his tanned face. "Quit? Quit the race?"

Kaye nodded and sipped her tea. She waited for the answer she expected, the decision that undoubtedly would follow.

But Matt looked beyond her and from deep within him, a resounding "Hell no, I won't quit!" exploded.

Kaye blinked and sat up straight. What was he saying?

Matt's arms were akimbo as he reasoned loudly. "Hell no, I'm not quitting! That man's still a crook! Gilbert Ashland has had free rein on this town too long! I'm still in the race. I may not win, but I'll give him a good run for it. And maybe . . . just maybe . . . cause some people around here to look beyond their nose!"

"Matt, are you sure you want to do this?" Kaye's voice was doubtful, knowing his lack of previous commitment to the endeavor.

He gazed at her steadily as ideas formed rapidly in his head. "If I don't do it, Kaye, then who will?"

She shook her head honestly. "No one."

Matt sat on the edge of the sofa, leaning enthusiastically toward her. "Kaye, if I continue in this race, I'll need everyone's help . . . Davis, Nan, and yours. Will you help me?"

"Mine?" Kaye laughed incredulously. "I'll support you, Matt, but I couldn't possibly help."

"Oh, yes you can. I have a plan. Davis can handle the money and be the campaign treasurer. But you . . . you can be my campaign manager." A smug, satisfied expression crossed his face.

Kaye was appalled. "Are you crazy? I don't know the first thing about campaigns . . . or politics!"

"You have all the skills you need. Come on, Kaye. You'd be perfect for it. And I'll show you what I need. You can also help me write the speeches. It would only entail scheduling a few events. Maybe take several evenings a week."

Kaye folded her arms. "No! I'm too busy! I have the shop—"

Matt took her hands and gently unfolded her arms. "Kaye, please. I need you. Don't you understand? I promise it won't take too much of your time. It won't interfere with your business. It may delay the opening of the shop a few weeks, but we'll help you with that. The race will be over in a month."

She shook her head. How would it affect her renting from Gil? "Matt, I'm not interested in getting involved in the politics of this town—"

He interrupted her protests. "What about me, Kaye? Are you interested in me? All right, Kaye. This is your chance to tell me to go to hell."

Instinctively she reached up, her slender hand caressing his face. "Matt, you know I can't do that. Of course, I care for you." She sighed heavily, gazing into those blue eyes of his, knowing she couldn't refuse him again. "All right," she agreed quietly. "I have to wait for my sales tax license before opening the shop, so I do have some time to spare. I'll help you if that's what you really want."

"Hot-damn! That's what I want to hear! All I need is a little support and help from my friends. If you and Davis and Nan will stand behind me, I can pull it off! I know I can!" He stood and gathered Kaye into his strong arms. Before she knew what was happening, she was clinging to his shoulders, swinging around, shrieking with glee, laughing with him . . . kissing him . . . rejoicing along with him!

She was lost in the warm desire of his kiss, forgetting about her vow to abstain. All she could think of was Matt's touch, his lips on hers, his obvious joy with her response, and it was wonderful! Kaye clutched his huge

86

sturdy frame. Here was someone she could lean on
. . . someone who would protect her . . . someone who
needed her as she needed him. And, as her passion rose
to match his, Kaye wanted him to love her, too.

Abruptly, he halted and, with a ragged sigh, slowly
lowered her feet to the floor. The only sound was that of
their breathing and the crackling of the fire. Kaye's arms
slid around his shoulders and down to rest on his chest.
Purposely, she moved them no further, for she delighted
in the masculine warmth she found there.

Matt's face was serious and his voice rather
raspy. "Kaye . . . I didn't intend for that to happen. I
shouldn't—"

Kaye's slender index finger compulsively outlined his
lips, quieting them. "You didn't, Matt. I did . . ." She was
acutely aware of her entire body leaning on his, her breasts
pushing against his muscular chest.

Matt, too, was conscious of her physical effectuation.
"Oh, God, Kaye, I can't stay away from you. I want you
so . . . ," he murmured.

The two of them stared long, agonizing minutes into
each other's eyes, silently acknowledging their desires. His
sapphire gaze asked the question she knew was burning
blatantly with his flaming passion. Matt had honestly
made his desires known from the beginning. But Kaye was
just starting to acknowledge hers. He had waited her out
and kissed away the facade . . . her armor, as he called it.
Oh, how she wanted him. Her limbs ached for the satisfaction that only he could give, and her arms pulled him
closer to her. Was this the answer he sought?

Slowly Matt bent his head to hers, kissing her moist,
waiting lips with such passion he took her breath away.
But Kaye wanted the breathless, magic time to last forever. His arms folded securely around her, and Kaye felt as
though she were a bird, soaring above the world to a

long-lost physical plane of ecstasy. She curved delightfully against him, confident that his strength would shore her in times of weakness. With him, she didn't have to be a tower of strength, and it was a relief.

Amazingly, he wanted her, even though he was aware of her fear of loving. He had returned to her although she had rejected him so acutely last week. Matt still offered himself as a wall on which she could lean and rest and gain strength for another day. Oh, she needed someone like him. She had needed him for a long, long time. But she hadn't even realized it until now.

Together, as one, they sank to the old braided rug on the floor in front of the fireplace. Their arms were wrapped tightly around each other, as if each was afraid of losing the other. And, indeed, they may have been.

Matt's lips left a sweet trail from Kaye's willing mouth to her flushed cheeks and her closed eyelids. Against her ear, his breath was hot and ragged. "Did I tell you what a miserable time I had in Miami without you?"

"I was lonely here without you," she admitted softly.

"Next time, you're going with me if I have to drag you along." He kissed her temple while his hands slipped to her hips, stroking her rounded buttocks.

"Next time . . ."—she opened her eyes and smiled reassuringly at him as she spoke haltingly—"you won't have to drag me along. I'll go willingly." There was a promise in the passionate glow in her bronze eyes.

"Kaye, my pretty lady, you are everything I want in a woman." His hand caressed each breast, moving sensuously over the covering of the silky robe, wanting to slide inside but not daring. He could feel the firmness of the rosy peaks hidden beneath the robe and knew Kaye was experiencing the beginnings of an awakening passion. Oh, how he longed to be the spark that ignited her smoldering embers. But, not too fast. It was only a few days ago that

88

she had broken into tears in his arms. He didn't want that to happen again. Although Matt desired her ardently, he wanted the feelings between them to be mutual. Tonight was the first time he really felt her active response. But he wanted more than that. He wanted her totally. She must desire him, too.

"Oh, Matt, please hold me," she murmured against his ear, sending erotic chills down his spine. Her skillful lips lit a path of fire from his jawline to the primitive throbbing in his neck to the soft cushion of feathery hair on his chest.

Kaye knew what she was doing to him, and it was maddening . . . and marvelous! Maybe this wasn't too soon, after all. She seemed so willing to accept his physical love . . . almost eager. Matt stretched out and, with an inner groan, his hands sketched her contours, molding her completely to him.

Kaye had just nestled comfortably against his chest when the two of them were abruptly pounced upon by a fluffy, wriggling, warm entity who touched them with a cold nose, then proceeded to further interrupt the quiet rapture of the evening.

"Oh, damn, Heidi—MOVE!" Kaye giggled, raising her head from Matt's muscular chest.

"Damn dog has the worst timing in the world! Do you have a porch or bathroom where I can lock the beast up?"

"Matt, no," Kaye protested, reaching across his prone chest to pet the happy animal.

He grabbed her hand, pulling it to the palpitations of his heart. "Feel that? I can't stand any more interruptions like that. It's bad for my health, lady. Come here. Things were just beginning to happen."

She plunged her hand inside his shirt and tickled his chest lightly with her stubby fingernails. Right now she wished those nails were long and sensual again! "Hey, things are still happening! Heidi's just doing her job. Protection, right?"

"Who was the idiot that brought that damn dog here in the first place?" Matt grumbled. "With me around, you don't need her protection anyway!"

Kaye sat up completely and looked down at Matt. "The same idiot who thinks I can be a campaign manager. Matt, I just don't know—Oh, oh, Heidi needs to go outside! Quick, the door—hurry, Matt!"

The magic moment between them was gone.

Both adults and the tiny dog scrambled for the door. Kaye continually praised Heidi, grateful for a brilliant act on the part of the animal. "She learns very fast. And she's just a baby, too! Isn't she smart, Matt? That's what she was trying to tell us all along."

"Hmmm, yeah, real smart. Just what I love to do: walk the dog in the middle of—"

"Well, it's better than cleaning up—"

"Okay, okay, I get the picture! Wonder if Davis wants another dog."

"Oh, no you don't, Matt Logan! Heidi's mine, now! We're a team. I need her . . . remember?"

He stuffed his hands in his pockets. "Well, I don't need her damned inconvenient interruptions! I only need you!"

Kaye slipped her arm around his waist and followed the pup back inside the warm house. "Well, you have us both, you lucky guy!"

Heidi curled contentedly on a corner of the rug while Matt and Kaye finished off the six-pack and discussed political strategy—Matt's future political career. He left her house, very late, with plans for the initial organizational meeting of the high-ranking members of his campaign set for the following night at Kaye's kitchen headquarters. That the high-ranking and low-ranking members were the same—and only—close friends he had in town, did not diminish the importance of the gathering. Win or lose, they would launch a fight this town and Gilbert Ashland wouldn't soon forget. *Win or lose? Why, WIN, of course!* They pledged their dedication to it.

At the door, Matt turned and slipped his big hand under Kaye's auburn hair to the warmest spot on her neck. "Lady . . ."—his voice was a husky whisper—"next time . . . next time, the dog goes out first."

She smiled, enjoying his touch as well as his teasing. It had been a long time since she had felt this lighthearted. "Next time? Sounds like a threat."

He moved closer and his masculine fragrance filled her senses. "There will be a next time. That's not a threat, pretty lady. That's a promise."

He kissed her smiling lips, and she watched him walk away with a lilt in her heart. Perhaps it was time to turn to love at last. Perhaps next time? Her heart skipped a beat and she closed the door with renewed hope.

CHAPTER FIVE

Kaye stood by the entrance, clipboard in hand, a smile plastered on her face. She had spent a hectic week organizing this hastily planned banquet. She marveled at the size of the crowd flocking into the school cafeteria for a catered twenty-five-dollar-a-plate barbeque and a chance to hear the handsome athlete who was candidate for mayor in tiny Twin Oaks. Curiosity was probably their main motivation —that was the calculation of the campaign committee. However, the curiosity was expected to be replaced by excitement after Matt's speech. It was rumored that he espoused new campaign promises and had hired an expensive speech writer from Dallas to spark up his speeches.

They had Nan to thank for the carefully planted rumors. She knew just who to tell. From the size of the crowd, the townspeople were anxious to hear the candidate and judge for themselves. And that's exactly what the Logan-for-Mayor Committee wanted!

Kaye turned toward Nan and Davis Chandler who worked speedily to reduce the crowd's long line by exchanging checks for tickets. Nan and Kaye had expressed doubts about Davis's ambitious money-making schemes, but the first of his numerous ideas seemed to be working. There were several others on the drawing board for the coming weeks, including opening Kaye's antique shop so that Matt could stage a public-invited ribbon cutting. Kaye was extremely satisfied with that plan. It meant they would all work to help her open the shop earlier than originally scheduled. Admittedly, the publicity wouldn't hurt her future business at all.

Her eyes scanned the buzzing crowd, searching for Matt. She spotted his curly blond hair and broad shoulders as he moved between tables, shaking hands with everyone, smiling, nodding, listening. With pride she noticed that he walked with barely a limp. He had worked hard to recuperate quickly from the knee surgery, so that wouldn't be a factor. And she hadn't heard him complain about being an *ex*-pro football player in several weeks. They had been too busy. In all fairness, the activity generated by the campaign had been good for her, too.

A faintly familiar, resonant male voice interrupted her musings. "Excuse me, miss. Could you direct me?"

Kaye snapped back to her task, looking squarely into the steel-gray eyes of Gilbert Ashland. "Oh . . . uh . . . let me see your ticket, sir. What a . . . nice surprise to see you here, Mayor Ashland."

"I thought we settled the business of names long ago. I'm Gil to you, Kaye. I might add, it's a surprise to see you here, too. And working in this man's campaign, as well." He gestured toward Matt's tall figure towering above the crowd.

"Uh, let's see, I think your seats are at this table on the far left. Are you . . . is Mrs. Ashland with you?" Kaye looked hopefully beyond him, but failed to see the flowing-gowned woman who usually graced his side.

Gil's silver-toned drawl resounded as he answered,

"Regretfully, no. Mrs. Ashland couldn't make it tonight. But I would count it as an honor if you'd sit with me, Kaye." He followed her to the table and stood by the chair she indicated, as if refusing to sit until she agreed to his sudden invitation.

But Kaye's answer was quick. "Oh, I can't. I mean, I'll be so busy tonight that I probably won't even have time to sit. I'm sorry, Mayor . . . er, Gil."

His hand touched her arm and slid down to her hand. "I hate to see you working so hard, my dear, especially for my opponent. Tell you what, I'll save this seat beside me just for you. If you have an opportunity, you can just slip right in here. I'd like to talk to you about your business."

Damn him! Gil knew she was sensitive about her business, and the fact that he owned the building left her feeling wary. Hesitantly, Kaye looked at the offending chair, realizing that Gil had maneuvered her into it. "Thank you, Gil. I'll make every effort to join you," she finished weakly. She would be back, and he knew it!

"Please do, Kaye. Surely, during the speech, you'll be finished with your part in this . . . this charade . . . and can join me."

"Ah, yes. Surely . . ." Kaye eased away with a sinking feeling inside. *During the speech!* It would be a stinging attack on the mayor's manipulation of funds—she knew every word because she wrote it! He certainly wouldn't be so eager for her company if he knew that she was the rumored, expensive speech writer!

Kaye assisted with seating the crowd, helped Davis drag out another folding table, and set it up for six. She checked with the kitchen staff—did they have enough food? How about coffee? And where were those roving mariachis she had hired? As the lights began to dim and the school auditorium took on a reasonable facsimile of a dining hall, she sought Matt. Reaching for his corded arm, she pulled him aside for a brief exchange.

"How's this for a spur-of-the-moment crowd?" she beamed.

He closed his hand over hers affectionately. "They must crave to hear someone besides Gil Ashland. All of you have done a super job getting this set up, Kaye. Now, it's up to me. How much do you think we've pulled in tonight?"

"Five thou easily. But half of it's spent already on ads and printouts. Plus this spread isn't free."

He shrugged. "If we break even, I'll be pleased."

"Maybe you'll be satisfied, but the committee won't be! We're doing this to pay the bills!"

"Hungry for that money, aren't you?" he teased. "See what a business head you've developed?"

She shrugged. "It's all your fault. If you hadn't persuaded me that you could win this election, I would be merrily selling my antiques."

"We're doing everything we can to make that a reality, too."

She nodded with a smile. "I know, and I appreciate it. Now, listen to me, Matt. There are a couple of things you should know. All of the county judges are here. They're seated to the center. Law enforcement, sheriff, and police chief are to the left. Those complimentary tickets paid off. And your illustrious opponent is to your right."

"Ashland's here?"

"Yep. Furthermore, he's asked that I sit with him during the speech."

Matt raised one eyebrow. "Why?"

She tried to shrug it off. "I don't know. He said something about talking about my business."

Suddenly Matt grinned devilishly. "Just don't tell him you wrote my speech! He may cancel your lease!"

Kaye shook her head. "I'm entirely innocent. I'm just a poor, ignorant, voluntary campaign worker."

Matt took a step closer. "Poor and volunteer, maybe. But ignorant—no way! And don't forget who you're going home with, pretty lady . . ."

Kaye's dark eyes met Matt's blue ones in a brief, intimate acknowledgment of his words. "Now, don't forget to talk slowly, pause for emphasis where we practiced, and smile at the beginning and the end. You have a marvelous smile, Matt. You'll win on that smile alone," she encouraged.

He shook his head, taking the job at hand seriously. "Oh, no, I won't. It'll take much more than a smile and a famous name. It will require the concerted effort of all of us, and I damn-well know it. Well, wish me luck."

"Don't forget your speech. Where are your notes? Oh, I think I see those damn roving mariachis—they've probably been roving the streets. Gotta go." Kaye paused and squeezed his hand. "Good luck, Matt," she whispered.

He winked. "See you later . . . and don't you forget it."

Kaye hurried over to direct the three sombrero-attired musicians. She refilled the coffeepot, checked briefly with Nan at the door, even inquired about the janitors to make sure they were available. She had done everything she could think of to delay the inevitable. Taking a deep breath, Kaye smoothed her prairie skirt and fluffed the ruffled blouse as she aimed for Gil's table.

Mayor Gilbert Ashland's lips curled into a triumphant smile, and he drawled eloquently, "Kaye, I'm so glad you could join us. Do you know Judge Ferris, the juvenile court judge, and his lovely wife Evie?" He gestured to the other couple. "Norris and Mrs. Johns. Helene, isn't it? Norris is the court administrator. This is Kathryn Coleman. She's a newcomer to our fine community and will be opening an antique shop on the square very soon, won't you, Kaye?" The introductions constituted a mini-speech as the mayor lost no opportunity for the spotlight.

Kaye exchanged niceties all around the table and tried to slide inconspicuously into the chair beside Gil.

Gil gave Kaye his full attention and blocked the inclusion of the others with the angle of his shoulders. "You look especially beautiful tonight, Kaye. I like your country dress with the ruffles and all. It's very feminine." His gray eyes roamed to her cleavage, which was framed by the gathered material of her pearly pink blouse.

Kaye shifted, knowing that from his viewpoint, he was admiring more than pink ruffles. "Thank you, Gil. This is a prairie skirt and blouse, a stylish tribute to the pioneer women's attire. It seemed appropriate."

"The color and style become you, Kaye." His gaze dipped to encompass her seated figure, then met her eyes boldly.

Her cheeks colored angrily, and Kaye felt sure from their tingling, they matched her blouse. "You wanted to discuss the business, Gil." She struggled to keep her voice even.

He smiled coldly. "Ah, yes. I am just curious, from a professional point of view, of course, when do you plan to be available for business, Kaye?"

"Oh, in just a few weeks I'll be open," Kaye smiled confidently. She took a bite of the potato salad, which quickly knotted in her stomach.

"Frankly, I had hoped you would be ready to open the doors to the public by now. I'm eager to see the town square full of attractions, you understand."

Especially when you own the buildings, Kaye thought viciously. But she managed a pleasant smile. "Surely you know that these things take time, Gil. I've been getting the shop ready with cleaning, rearranging counters, and building additional storage shelves. I'm in the process of

97

acquiring a cash register and a couple of glass showcases. Then, of course, I have to do some additional buying."

"Where do you buy antiques these days?" he asked.

Kaye sipped the coffee and shuddered as the strong brew hit her nervous stomach. "Back East. In fact, I'm returning to Delaware this weekend for an estate auction." *There,* she confirmed silently. *That should satisfy his infernal curiosity about the shop.* Kaye looked around for a waiter and, catching his attention, asked, "Could I have tea, please?"

"Make that two. This coffee is awfully strong, isn't it, Kaye?" Gil leaned closer as he spoke. Even though the visible upper part of his body was a reasonable distance from her, his legs remained close to hers and even brushed against her thigh occasionally.

By the time the first course was completed, she was furious with the audacity of the man and would have left his company except for the fear of causing a scene and ruining Matt's successful evening. So Kaye remained, despising every minute she had to endure Gil Ashland.

Just as the lights dimmed again and the carefully planned spotlight centered on the podium, the waiter plopped two glasses of tea on the table before them. *Iced tea,* she thought miserably. *I should have known! These Texans only know about iced tea!* She sipped it anyway, longing for her own warm, spicy brew and this evening to end.

Kaye sat politely, eyes glued to Matt, as he lit into the mayor's financial policies, touching on the park that was never actualized, abandoned policemen's pensions, and the deplorable conditions of the detention center. During the scathing attack, various guttural noises were barely discernible from the incumbent, but Kaye blandly ignored them. She noted, instead, the exchange of glances and nods of approval from the crowd.

By the end of the evening, Gil was in such an over-wrought state that he bid her a hasty "Good evening."

Kaye smiled her adieu and heaved a grateful sigh of relief. She had managed to survive both Gil Ashland and the banquet.

Afterward, the campaign committee of four gathered around Kaye's kitchen table to analyze the evening and plan the next event. They munched chips and drank Texas beer, made from fresh spring water. It was delicious, and spirits ran high.

"Hot-damn! I can't believe the size of the crowd tonight! And their positive response! It was fantastic!" Matt's sapphire eyes twinkled with his exhilaration.

Davis was more droll. "I can't believe you've learned to make a speech in a week!" He clapped his old buddy on the back and laughed. "You gave 'em something to think about tonight, Matt. Now, that's what I call a REAL political speech! Give 'em some punch! And a little hell!"

"I have Kaye to thank for that. She's a regular drill sergeant when it comes to perfection. We've done nothing all week, except work on that goddamn speech! *Nothing!*" Matt's tone was sarcastic, but the teasing was apparent in his blue eyes.

Kaye countered defensively. "A crash course in speech-making takes concerted effort on the part of the teacher as well as the student, Mr. Candidate. I'll agree it was grueling. But, you have to admit, it paid off. At least, all of you got to sit back and enjoy the speech. Meanwhile, I agonized over every word and, at the same time, had to sit beside the incumbent and listen to his grumbling. I will say, however, it was the only time I've seen Gil Ashland speechless!"

Pausing in her laughter, Nan asked, "What did he say about Matt's attack?"

Kaye shrugged with a triumphant laugh. "He growled

99

under his breath with every scathing word, but I just ignored him!"

Howls of laughter shook the walls of the old house as the four took delight in Kaye's accounts of Gil's reactions. The noise disturbed Heidi, who roused and gazed around sleepily at the rambunctious group. Then, she settled herself on the old braided rug again, remembering that the place was usually loud and boisterous when her mistress's friends were there.

"Frankly, I think Nan's rumor did the trick to pull in the curious." Kaye grinned. "They wanted to know what a high-priced speech writer sounded like!"

"And, what is your price, Ms. Anonymous Speech Writer?" Matt teased.

Kaye grinned sassily. "My price is so high that I have to volunteer my services, Mr. Candidate! This two-bit operation certainly can't afford me!"

"Oh ho, Kaye! Well-spoken!" applauded Nan. "Hey, speaking of money, would you like to know how much we made tonight?"

"Yes!" they enjoined.

"Well, after all of our expenses are paid, the remainder is four thousand, one hundred dollars! How's that?" Nan announced proudly.

"Is that all?" Kaye was the only one who seemed disappointed.

"Is that all! I think that's pretty good," admitted Nan.

"I guess I was expecting much more from this evening," Kaye explained with a shrug. "But it's a good start."

"Here," Nan offered. "Take a look at the list of expenses."

They studied the accounts and discussed the upcoming luncheon with the Ladies' Auxiliary.

Finally, Nan yawned and stood up. "I don't know about you-all, but I'm beat. Ready to go, Davis?"

"You bet," he agreed and lumbered toward the door. They all exchanged farewells and congratulations for the evening.

"I'll walk you out," Matt offered.

With the tensions of the evening relieved, pangs of hunger gripped Kaye. She waited, but Matt seemed to be taking his time, so she proceeded to scramble a couple of eggs. When Matt eventually returned, he was heaving a huge white furry roll over his shoulder.

"What in the world is that?" Kaye exclaimed. Even Heidi jumped up and started barking at the strange contraption he carried.

"Hush, animal!" Matt fussed at the pup. "And move over! This place in front of the fireplace is reserved!" He began to unroll the white thing in the chosen spot, assessing the irregular shape, rearranging it to a more suitable position, then standing back to admire his addition to the room. "There! How do you like it? Personally, I think it makes the room."

"Makes the room *what?*" Kaye laughed, somewhat skeptical of the prospect of the plush, inviting rug sprawled in front of her fireplace.

"Whatever we want it to be, Kaye. It's just for you and me. Don't you like it?"

"Oh, of course, Matt. It is beautiful. What . . . what kind of fur is it?" She still kept her distance.

"Fur?" he repeated incredulously, leaning toward the dramatic. He turned his mocking tones to the pup who sniffed curiously at the new rug that had replaced the familiar braided mat. "The lady is full of East Coast charm and poise, but shows her ignorance of fine western design and crafts!"

Kaye laughed aloud at his antics. "All right, Tex, what is it? We both give up!"

Matt's drawl was deep and affected. "This is gen-u-wine

101

sheepskin, ma'am. I ordered it from New Mexico, hoping I could persuade you to make love on it here in front of the fire. Sounds like fun, doesn't it? Come over here and feel it. Of course, the best way to test its softness is completely nude!"

"Nude? Matt!"

"Yes, naked! No clothes! That way you can feel it with your entire body! Have you ever tried it?"

She giggled at the very erotic notion and shook her head negatively.

Matt stood with arms akimbo, his muscular form outlined against the glow of the fire. "Then, why not try it now, Kaye?"

The question was blatantly sensuous, and Kaye's body tingled anxiously as she considered his words. Sometimes, Matt's honest, suggestive statements stimulated her in ways that had remained dormant since the death of her husband. Her reactions were disconcerting, for there were times that Kaye felt she couldn't resist Matt's masculine appeal if he touched her once more. Tonight was one of those times. She lifted the plates she had been preparing and tried to laugh away his invitation. "I can enjoy the beauty of it like this. Are you hungry?" Slowly she approached him, a small plate of scrambled eggs with toast in each hand. "I . . . I couldn't eat at the banquet. Too nervous, I guess. Now, I'm hungry. Would you like something?" She smiled and handed him a plate. "We could sit here." She sank to the soft area beneath her feet and ran her fingers through the pliant fibers.

He took the offered plate from her and shrugged. "It's not exactly what I had in mind, but . . ." He sprawled on the rug beside her.

"Eat your eggs before they get cold." Suddenly she realized how absolutely ridiculous she sounded.

"How can you think of food at a time like this?"

Kaye giggled nervously. "The truth is, I'm trying to divert your attention!"

"Trying to give me the brush-off is probably more correct!" Matt took a bite of the egg. "Hey, not bad for a city gal! What's the magic ingredient here?"

She smiled. "See? It didn't take much to change your interest. They say the way to a man's heart is through his stomach. A little cream cheese works wonders with ordinary scrambled eggs." She sampled her own preparation, then nodded with approval.

"What would you know about 'ordinary,' my classy lady? I'll concede, though, you've already found the way to this man's heart! And that's not all! But, we can nibble our way to love, if that's what pleases you!"

She laughed at his brazen offers. "You're dreadful! But definitely a challenge! And the rug . . . is beautiful and very sensuous."

"Glad to hear you admit it." Matt grinned as he gathered their plates and deposited them on the hearth. "Tit-a-latin' is the word, ma'am! Sure beats that damned old worn-out braided thing. Softer, too. Want to try it out?"

Kaye looked at him tentatively, remembering their last embrace on that old rug. In the silence that followed, each recalled that kiss . . . and the promise that followed. The avowed moment was *now*, and they both sensed it. *Knew it.*

"Well?" He was beside her, tempting her senses with his very presence. His virility. Oh, God, his magnetic appeal.

"Matt . . . I . . ." Her brown eyes were large and expressive.

His tone was that of frustration. "Kaye, my God! Don't look at me with such a frightened expression. I won't attack you! But I'm a normal man, and you're a very desirable woman. I want you . . . more than I've ever wanted any woman. I believe you are a lady who likes to be loved . . . and to love. I want to be the one to kindle those fires that are smoldering within you."

Kaye quivered at his words. Matt had been so patient with her, and still she denied her deepest feelings. This man . . . this muscular, kind, giant of a man near her aroused deep passions that she had been unwilling to admit. *Until now.* Did he know what was happening to her? What he was doing to her? Could he read it in her eyes? Would he believe her if she denied this yearning, this lust? She smiled faintly. "You are the only one who could . . ."

Matt's large hand slid around her neck, nestling in the thick auburn hair. "I want you, Kaye. I want to feel your body next to mine . . . your arms around me . . ." His lips descended to hers, kissing, caressing, soothing until she instinctively returned it with arousing activity of her own. Lost in desire's immediate response, Kaye was unaware that she was meeting the gratifying pressure of his lips with her own force. She met his tongue sweetly, then allowed it easy entry to probe her willing mouth with sensuous, pulsating movements. Instinctively, she arched against him, as dormant desires raged through her body.

He molded her curves to his male hardness, relishing the soft femininity of her open, responsive body next to him. Matt sighed with pleasure. She would be his tonight! He had claimed her and, now, they both plummeted toward the ultimate.

With a soft moan, Kaye clamored for control, realizing the closeness of her own eager submission. She tried to heave herself away from his steellike clutches. "Matt . . . oh, Matt . . ."

He raised his head above hers, bewildered by her sudden reluctance. "Kaye . . . don't deny your emotions," he rasped thickly. "You want me as badly as I want you . . . you know it's true."

104

"No—" she lied. How long could she deny these feelings that flooded her being with warmth? One touch of his hands . . .

He cupped her face, his fingers trailing down both sides of her neck. "I see a beautiful woman who is denying her own inner feelings." He feathered kisses on her hair, cheeks, quivering lips. They trailed lightly down her awakening body as his lips sought the pulsating warmth at the sensitive hollow of her neck. The fiery touch of his lips on her soft skin sent pangs of longing through her, igniting small flames of desire.

Her arms clasped fiercely around his muscular shoulders and, with eyes tightly shut, she laid her head against his chest. "Matt, you're right. I want you to love me. But, I'm feeling so mixed up. I . . . I came out here to Texas to escape, not to . . ." She groped for the right words.

"Find joy? Don't feel guilty for being happy again, Kaye."

She opened her eyes and looked at him, her arms still resting on him, drawing from his strength. "I guess I am feeling a little guilty."

"You can't expect to live alone, cold and unhappy, for the rest of your life. Don't let that happen. It's not good for you. Life's too short to waste it in a lonely, unfulfilled existence. Oh, Kaye, darling, let me love you . . ." His voice ended in an urgent whisper.

Kaye's head whirled with his words. He had said what she wanted—*needed*—to hear and yet, she didn't. She yearned for him . . . and she didn't! She wanted him to love her . . . but held back. Why?

Her eyes turned from Matt to the merrily blazing fire. Its warmth invaded her . . . encouraging, enchanting, enhancing the mood . . . until she sought Matt's passion-darkened eyes. She nodded, her brown eyes large and liquid.

Deliberately, he took her hands and kissed each palm, his eyes never leaving hers, his lips sending sensuous messages down her arms.

"You're shaking," he observed.

"I can't help it," she apologized. "I want this to be good."

Gently, he offered, "Let me make it good for both of us."

His hands encased her shoulders and firmly pushed her back until she sank into the soft depths of the rug. Kaye looked up at him expectantly, her mahogany hair fanning out to frame her head. "I see a very beautiful woman . . . one who is denying her real emotions . . . one who is hiding her desires."

She smiled wanly. "But not tonight, Matt."

With skillful, loving hands, he proceeded to stroke her entire length. First, he pushed her hair back from her forehead, then he traced her cheeks, outlined her lips and nose with a steady finger. Instead of joining her length on the rug, he continued to sit beside her, talking, soothing, caressing. "Close your eyes, Kaye, and enjoy."

And she did.

Matt's fingers massaged her temples, spread through her hair to her scalp, then wandered behind her ears and down her neck. He felt the wild pulsating there, and bent to kiss the throbbing hollow. She shuddered visibly as he buried a kiss in her cleavage. His hands cupped each quivering mound, ringing the firm tips that hid beneath her ruffled blouse. As she felt the inevitable response of her nipples puckering under his manipulations, her eyes flew open.

"These are the reactions of a very sensuous woman, Kaye," he explained thickly, *as if she needed any telling!* "The problem is . . . these damned ruffles."

His hands moved and, in an instant, her blouse and bra

fell open, revealing the glow of her creamy breasts in the firelight.

"Oh, Kaye . . ." He bent to rain kisses from her eyelids to her slightly parted lips to the pulsing hollow of her throat to her waiting breasts. The tips grew firmer as his warm tongue flickered over each one, eliciting a soft moan from Kaye's throat. She reached for his shoulders, instinctively pulling him down to her.

"Not yet, Kaye, not yet . . ." His hand slipped under her full skirt to touch the warmth of her silken thighs.

She gasped at his electrifying touch. "The real problem is . . . these damned clothes!"

"You're right. Let's do something about it!"

In unspoken agreement, they tore eagerly at the encumbrances that kept them apart. Kaye's pink ruffled blouse was quickly discarded; then she shifted, sliding the skirt and panty hose over her hips with little effort. She relished in the luscious feel of the sheepskin under her nude skin. Stretching out, hands laced under her head, she watched Matt shed his clothes. With feminine curiosity, she admired his broad shoulders, the blond hair that curled on his chest, then disappeared below his belt. His waist was trim and muscles rippled in his back as he bent to discard his shoes and socks. With an inner smile, she acknowledged that he was certainly a marvelous specimen of masculinity. Then, it dawned on her that she was expected to go to bed with this man . . . and satisfy him! By the time he unzipped his slacks, the obvious realization of his arousal sent tingles of panic shooting up her limbs, to settle in a scared knot in the pit of her stomach.

What in the world was wrong with her? After all, she had been married. She was no young schoolgirl. And she was a consenting partner tonight. Why this sudden trepidation?

He turned to her, proud of his masculinity, eager to satisfy his longing. *Oh, dear God . . .*

Kaye's brown eyes widened as he lay on his side beside her on the soft, white rug. "Matt—" she faltered, her heart pounding heavily. "Matt . . . I—"

His hand settled on her waist, drawing slow circles on her sensitive flesh, moving slowly up her side to nestle under her soft breast. "Oh, Kaye, I've waited so long for this moment . . . for you."

Her hand grasped his wrist. "Matt, I have something to tell you."

The gentle caressing stopped abruptly. He spoke hesitantly. "Is it the wrong time for you—"

"Oh, no!" Her voice quivered and she shook her head reassuringly.

He propped up on one elbow so he could see her face. "Then, what?" His hand moved to enclose her breast possessively.

She let her gaze briefly encompass his nude form. "You won't laugh?" Kaye wanted to cry—and run away from all this!

His hand caressed her soft flesh comfortingly. "Laugh? Of course not! What's wrong, Kaye?" He tickled the smooth skin of her belly, ever so lightly, delighting in her satiny warmth.

She licked her lips and gazed seriously into his eyes. His desire was evident as his firm body pressed closer to her, and she knew there was no turning back. Soon she wouldn't want to! "I'm . . . I'm nervous."

Relief flooded Matt's face. This, he could handle. His eyes were gentle and sincere. "Don't be nervous. I won't hurt you, Kaye." He made small circles that wound delicately around her thigh. Kaye trembled at the delicious sensation and found herself mesmerized by Matt's gently wandering touch. Suddenly, she tensed and Matt looked at her with a question in his eyes.

"Oh, Matt." She managed a smile. "I don't know what's wrong with me. It's just been so long . . ."

"It's been way too long for us." His hand caressed the warm curve of her hip as he talked. "Kaye, my beautiful, beautiful lady . . . I want to love you. I want you . . . desire you completely. But, I want your love, Kaye, as I love you." His kiss sealed the statement while fiery hands sought her hidden feminine desires.

His words left her stunned . . . *as I love you.* Love? Did she love him? Could she respond to him like this if she didn't? Deep inside, Kaye thrilled at the thought. "Oh, Matt . . . I want your love. I want you . . . now."

With an eager groan, he shifted his impassioned body to hers, over hers, igniting the flames of her long-dormant passions. "Kaye . . . I'll be gentle when I love you . . ."

And gentle he was.

His lips softly teased the slopes of her breasts, his tongue leaving a trail of passion as he suckled her yearning flesh. She forgot her nervousness, she forgot everything, as she surrendered to pure sensations and the joy of his love. Matt sensed her new eagerness and delighted in the feel of her love-warmed body relaxing into his as they melted together against the sensuous softness of the sheepskin rug.

As they basked in the fire's glow, Kaye looked into Matt's eyes and saw such tenderness and passion in their sparkling depths that she needed no further verbal declarations of his love, and instead let their bodies speak their secrets with timeless gestures and caresses. Matt nestled his face in the warm curve of her neck, pressing heated kisses on the satiny flesh he savored so completely.

Kaye trailed her fingertips over the strength of his

shoulders, treasuring the feel of every hard-muscled inch of his incredibly soft skin. Pressing her palms into his trembling back, she moved her hands in tantalizingly slow strokes up and down his spine and was rewarded with a torrent of blazing kisses up the smooth column of her throat.

Feeling she had to bring Matt closer, ever closer, Kaye arched her slim, soft body to meet Matt's hard, virile strength. And, in an eruption of molten fire, they blazed together as one. It was exquisite!

Afterward, Matt held her tenderly in his big arms, cuddling her as they relaxed on the soft white rug in front of the fire. They held each other quietly, not disturbing the beauty of the moments with words. The flames had dwindled to red glowing coals, occasionally crackling to punctuate the silence.

When Matt finally spoke, his voice was low. "When will you be back, Kaye?"

"The auction is Saturday. I'll fly back Sunday evening." She paused, then added as an afterthought, "I have friends to see in Wilmington."

He sighed quietly, but she sensed his uneasiness about something.

"Matt?"

"Are you . . . coming back?"

She sat upright and looked at him. "Of course I'm coming back here. This is my home. Especially *now*."

His voice was thick with emotion and he reached for her. "Oh, God, Kaye. I don't want to lose you!"

"You won't lose me, Matt." Now it was her turn to reassure him. She wrapped an arm tightly around his bare waist and cushioned her head on the soft hair on his chest.

Matt's huge arms embraced her, pressing her vigorously to his broad chest. "Kaye, my beautiful lady, we've just begun . . . and ours will be a wonderful love."

"I'll return to your arms, Matt. I promise," she murmured sleepily and nestled comfortably in the security of his arms. She loved the sound of his words, cherished the assurance of his pledge. She dozed . . . content in the promise of their wonderful love.

CHAPTER SIX

A bitter arctic blast welcomed Kaye when she deplaned at Wilmington, Delaware. She had forgotten how harsh the winters were in the East, spoiled by only two months in balmy Texas. Cringing against the biting wind, she was immediately engulfed into Hal's waiting arms.

"Kathryn! Over here—out of the wind!" He ushered her away from the door and the crowd.

"Hal! How wonderful to see you!"

"Kathryn, I'm so glad you came back! This is where you belong, you know. Ah, Kathryn, you look marvelous!" His hands were on her elbows, but she could feel their grip through her heavy coat.

"So do you, Hal." Unexpectedly, her eyes misted. There was something about going back again and seeing familiar faces that touched her deeply. Also, a certain look on Hal's face told her what she didn't want to know—to admit.

They stood gazing face-to-face, as if mesmerized by each other for long, blissful moments. Her smile was glorious, her cherry cheeks lit by a touch of the Texas sun.

Hal's clear blue eyes took in the healthy glow of her skin, the coppery highlights in her wind-tossed hair, the happiness sparkling in her mahogany eyes. He took a deep breath, as if to inhale the classic essence of the lovely woman before him.

"I must admit," he finally spoke, "Texas has been good for you. You look . . . absolutely beautiful, Kathryn."

"Thank you, Hal."

"The place is just not the same without you, my dear. Ah, Kathryn . . . I've missed you."

Suddenly, she was Kathryn Coleman again. Not Kaye. And she wasn't in Texas. She was back in Delaware—and it felt nice.

"I've missed you, too, Hal. And everything here," she admitted huskily as a million memories flashed before her eyes. Kathryn raised her oval face to him, and Hal kissed her cheek conservatively. Yes, he was still the same dear, sweet Hal.

He looked quickly at the crowd, then back to Kaye. "Come on, dear, let's get your luggage." Hal steered her down the busy hall. "Quite honestly, Kathryn, I had my doubts about you actually returning until I saw you getting off that plane."

She hurried to keep up with his long strides. "Why, Hal, I told you I'd be here. Why shouldn't I?"

He paused and looked at her. "I don't know. Just a feeling, I guess. Perhaps it was my own fear that I wouldn't see you again."

"Of course, you'll see me again. We're old friends, aren't we? Next time, I want you to come to Texas."

His nod was jerky, and he continued walking.

Kaye rushed to explain. "Hal, I'm so glad you called to tell me about the auction. It's just perfect for my new business. And timing couldn't be better. It's impossible to get good antiques in Texas these days."

"Well, I don't know much about antiques, but when I learned of this auction, I thought of you. It seemed a good excuse to get you back."

She smiled at his admission. "Well, I don't know much about auctions, so we're even. Actually, I was delighted to have an excuse to get away. I've been so busy lately. And, since this trip is business, it's tax deductible. Thanks to you, Hal, I know about those things!"

"You seem happy, Kathryn." Hal marveled at the light dancing once again in her eyes.

"I am," she assured him. And, basking in last night's memories of Matt's loving arms, she was elated. There was an inner glow she just couldn't hide.

They stood near the baggage counter. "Then, you like Texas?" There was an apprehension in his voice that she chose to ignore.

"I love it," she affirmed, with an enthusiastic smile. The statement was followed by an uneasy silence, so Kaye attempted to salvage the moment. "Hal, thanks for meeting me at the airport. I hope I haven't inconvenienced you."

"Of course not. I wouldn't miss this opportunity to see you for the world, Kathryn. I have been looking forward to this weekend." He easily hefted the suitcase she indicated.

"Now, Hal," Kaye said firmly. "You do not have to entertain me this weekend. I'm perfectly capable of getting around in this town. Just put me up in the DuPont Hotel, and I'll get a cab whenever I need to travel."

He stopped walking and answered with such resolve she had to smile. "A hotel? Like hell you will! You're staying with me, Kathryn! Stella is anxious to see you again and delighted at the prospect of having another woman in the house. And so am I."

"Stella? How is she? And are you keeping Reuben

114

busy?" She smiled at the thought of Hal's housekeeper and gardener. They were an older couple who fell in love while working for him. They had recently married, and Hal had hosted their wedding in the garden.

"They're fine. They've agreed to stay in the downstairs bedroom while you're here." He led her toward the glass exit doors.

"Oh, I'm not worried about that, Hal. I just don't want you, or Stella and Reuben, to go to any trouble while I'm here." Hal was so damned principled, he would probably be appalled to know she had slept with a man last night!

Hal halted by the door before they battled the driving wind again. "Kathryn, apparently you don't understand. I've reserved the entire weekend for you. I'll be taking you to the auction because that's what I want to do. Perhaps we can have a couple of enjoyable evenings out, unless, of course, you have plans to the contrary."

She blinked at his proposal. "I have no plans other than the auction."

"Well, then, it's settled. Tonight we have tickets for *Same Time, Next Year* at the University of Delaware. I hear this performance is fantastic. How does that sound?"

Kaye nodded agreeably. "Sounds great!"

"Come on, then. Reuben's waiting!" Hal motioned, and Kaye could see Reuben standing beside the tan Mercedes-Benz.

She was quickly ushered into the sumptuous velour and leather-covered backseat where they were able to continue their conversation. While Reuben maneuvered the classic vehicle across town, Kaye had the distinct feeling of being propelled into an entirely different world—a world she had abandoned. But, did she really belong here? Hal thought so.

His voice intruded in her musings. "Tomorrow, the auction will keep us busy all day. I have a catalogue of the

115

items for sale with estimates of their value. You should study that tonight, Kathryn. Then, we'll attend the presale exhibition in the morning. The auction begins at one."

"Hal, I'm impressed. I thought you didn't know anything about auctions and antiques," Kaye said admiringly.

"Thanks to you I'm learning, Kathryn," Hal admitted with a grin. "By tomorrow night, I assume we'll both be exhausted, so I have a quiet dinner planned. Just the two of us. Remember that little seafood place near New Castle?"

Fond memories flooded her as Kaye acquiesced willingly to Hal's arrangements for them. "You know how I love seafood, Hal. And it's been so long since I've had fresh shrimp or crab. It sounds marvelous!"

He sighed. "Also, several friends want to see you before you leave town. They've planned a Sunday brunch at the Copeland's. Betsy insisted . . ." Hal shrugged, as if apologizing. "I'm afraid it doesn't leave you much time to relax."

"Actually, Hal, it all sounds just wonderful!" Kaye admitted enthusiastically. "I'm anxious to see all of our old friends, too. And I know they want to hear about my new life in Texas. I have a few Texas tall tales for them!" She paused and placed her hand on his arm. "I just feel like I'm monopolizing your entire weekend, though."

He slipped his arm around her shoulders and pulled her close. His lips caressed her fragrant hair. "Believe me, Kathryn, I wouldn't have it any other way."

Hal was the perfect gentleman as he escorted her that evening to the university to see *Same Time, Next Year.* Kaye laughed and cried and couldn't help wondering if she and Hal would end up like the characters of the play— meeting once each year.

After the play, Kaye and Hal sipped café au lait and nibbled delectable French pastry in a dark, smoky coffee shop in Newark. The place was filled with university students. Many of the men had beards; the women wore their hair long and straight. Dress was casually preppy with button-down shirts, sweaters tied around shoulders, and Weejuns—no boots and no jeans. Music was slow jazz, not country-western.

The obvious contrast in life-styles turned her thoughts toward Texas. Wistfully, she wondered what Matt was doing tonight. With a small sigh, she realized that even though she had been away from him for only a few hours, she missed him. They were only a few flight hours, two thousand miles, but worlds apart! His words of love haunted her . . . did he really mean them? Did she want that? Was she ready for love?

"Ready to go, Kathryn?"

She jumped and looked up into Hal's intense eyes. "Oh, . . . yes. Hal, I have really enjoyed this evening. It's been marvelous to be back." Admittedly, she had missed this Eastern culture.

They were quiet on the way home. Hal had decided to drive the smaller, more intimate Porsche, and now they sped through the city on smooth, magic wheels. Indeed, it felt wonderful to be back in Delaware again, luxuriating in comfort with Hal and enjoying the cultural offerings. Was this really where she belonged?

They paused in the marbled entryway of Hal's two-story home. The moment was clumsy and silent. Then, Kaye smiled tiredly. "Thank you for a lovely evening, Hal." She squeezed his hand and walked away, feeling there was more to be said by them both. But not tonight.

So, Hal stood alone under the elegant crystal chandelier as Kathryn climbed the stairs alone. Oh, God, how he wanted to follow her!

Saturday was an exhausting, yet exhilarating day. It

117

was Kaye's first auction, and Hal helped her assess the values and bid properly. "Be discreet, Kathryn. No arm-waving Statue of Liberty bids. That advertises you as a novice. This is the standard method. If you want to jump the bid, motion with your fingers." He showed her the proper hand motions. "This is the covert catalogue-flip bid. You may prefer that, Kathryn."

She laughed at his demonstrations. "I didn't realize that bidding was such an art. Thanks for the instructions. I'll try not to embarrass you, Hal. In case I forget which is jumping or covert, will you be close by?"

"I'll be right with you, all day." And he kept his word; he was by her side the entire day.

By evening Kaye was very tired, and a quiet dinner was just what she needed. Hal knew her well enough to realize it. He was so good for her. Muted lights and easy-listening music drifted among the chandeliers and candles, enhancing the mood for lobster thermidor and Chablis Grenouilles. The light French wine was just right, and left Kaye relaxed as they skimmed home in his expensive car. She leaned her head back on the contoured velour headrest and enjoyed familiar sights along the Delaware River, the historic town of New Castle, and tree-lined boulevards of Wilmington.

As the Porsche slid into the driveway, Kaye was afforded another view of Hal's beautiful house at night. Muted lights from several strategic locations gave the two-story colonial an inviting, elegant appearance. The garage doors opened magically with the push of a button, and Hal and Kaye entered the house through the den.

"Have a seat, Kathryn. Relax. You look tired." He motioned while he walked around the bar to pour them a small Kahlúa stinger.

"I am tired, but it's a good feeling. I'm so pleased with the auction." Kaye approached the cold, black fireplace.

118

Above it were ribbons, awards, and pictures from the past. It was inevitable that she and Emery were in one of those photos somewhere, but she didn't even look for it. She didn't really want to be reminded; that was in the past. And Kaye was tired of reliving it. She had a future now, and she looked forward to it.

Hal stood very near, handing her the small, etched crystal. "Won't you have a seat, so we can talk?"

She sipped the dark liqueur and shook her head. "I've been sitting too much today. Ah, this Kahlúa is wonderful! In fact, this whole day—no, the weekend—has been terrific!" She walked around the room, observing photos and other appointments she remembered.

"Kathryn, just being with you again has been a joy for me." He watched her pensively, and Kaye sensed that he had more to say. Tonight would be the time to say it.

"Hal, how can I ever thank you? The auction was such a success for me. I found some primitives, a few pieces from the Shaker period, and a wooden dough box in excellent condition! None of those are available in Texas, and I'm so pleased."

He smiled at her enthusiasm. "I thought, for a while, that you'd buy up the whole lot."

"It was fun! Much more fun than regular buying! Wasn't it?"

"Yes," he admitted. How could he dispute her? She was right, and, oh, so alluring. "I'll keep you posted if I hear of another auction."

"Great! Just give me a call. Now," she sighed, "I've got to hire someone to haul my treasures back to Texas."

He propped his foot on the brick hearth. "I can get someone trustworthy around here. Let me take care of that, Kathryn."

She smiled gratefully. "Okay, Hal. You always take

care of things, don't you?" He was close, and she caught his expensive, spicy fragrance.

Quietly he admitted, "I hate to see you leave so soon."

"It has been a marvelous weekend, hasn't it?" She tried to turn away, but those captivating eyes of his held her steadfast.

"Kathryn, I want you to know how much I care for you."

"Oh, Hal." A tiny, nervous laugh escaped. "I know that. And I care for you, too." She didn't want this conversation to go any further.

"Kathryn, my dear, I wish you would let me take care of you. I would consider it a pleasure . . . an honor."

She laughed nervously again. "Let's not rehash that, Hal. Anyway, I can take care of myself just fine."

He cradled her hand in his, examined it, then held it up for her eyes. "Do you know how it hurts me to see your lovely hands like this? You've been working hard, Kathryn. And I'm just sick to see you doing this to yourself."

"Hal, a little hard work has never hurt anyone. These nails will grow back." She wondered frantically where Stella and Reuben were. They were supposed to be in the house this weekend, but she had hardly seen them. Where in hell were they tonight? She and Hal seemed to be entirely alone in the enormous house.

He kissed her hand, her knuckles, her fingertips, his lips making velvet trails over her abused skin. For a moment, she felt like a princess, enjoying, in spite of herself, his tender affection. His voice was low and gentle. "I would never let your hands look like this, Kathryn. I would pamper you, your hands, your whole body."

She gulped, knowing that he meant it. It would be marvelous if—

"Don't you want to be pampered again, Kathryn?"

120

She blinked—or was it a nod? He was so close, his breath fell hot on her face, his hand caressed her arm. "Hal, please—" she managed, before his lips claimed hers.

She thought first of the liqueur glass she held. To spill it would be embarrassing. But then, he held one too, didn't he? If so, then how was he gripping her so tightly? His hands, traveling sensuously down her back, pressed her to his firm body. He felt just as she expected, lean, well muscled, virile. His arms locked her to him; it was useless to resist. His thighs, hardened by years of jogging, were taut against hers. As her hips were impelled to mold tightly to his, she became acutely aware of his masculine arousal. She flushed hotly at the realization! Somehow, she never thought of Hal in sexual terms. Now, there was no avoiding the fact.

His lips caressed hers sweetly, played with them, tested her response. She felt the teasing tingle of his tongue on her lips and its light pressure on her teeth. Then, the sure exploration of her entire mouth sent tiny gasps to her throat. Had she opened up for him? While she pondered the thought, his tongue met hers, and conquered its weak resistance, plunging deeply into the crevices of her mouth. Should she allow this? Would Hal stop if she resisted? She tightened her mouth, making a smaller O. He mistook her action and continued with a slow, pulsating motion.

Oh, my God! Now, what? She felt suddenly very hot—nervously hot! This was not what she expected . . . wanted . . . from Hal. She had attempted to discourage him, but each effort had been misinterpreted and acted upon, eagerly!

Hal wanted her! There was no mistaking his intentions. He had made overtures, and she had responded accordingly. *Stupid! You fool!* she castigated herself. Her inexperience had plunged her into this predicament! Now, how did she get herself out? What should she do? Bite his tongue? Oh, dear God! She didn't dare! But, what? Within another few minutes she would be on her back!

Then, she would surely spill the liqueur! A small, helpless moan escaped her. Strange what she was thinking while Hal's tongue plunged her sensuously. His entire body was aroused against her, and all she could think of was how to avoid spilling her drink!

Suddenly, her mouth was free! Upon leaving her lips, he nibbled a tingling trail of kisses down the white column of her neck. He sought the sensitive hollow at her throat, and lower. At last, Kaye caught her breath and tried to gather her senses. "Hal—" she rasped. "Hal, please . . . don't!"

Slowly, he stopped kissing, touching, caressing her. Her feeble resistance was beginning to sink in. She was not responding. He understood. Sadly, he straightened. "Kathryn, I'm sorry—" His voice was thick, his breathing labored.

"Please, don't explain," she begged softly.

"I must. Kathryn, I'm not sure when I knew. But, it seems like I've loved you forever."

She looked down. "Don't, Hal. Please, don't say it."

"Why don't you want to hear that I love you, Kathryn?"

She shook her head, not wanting to tell him, not knowing what to say.

"You don't love me." His voice was flat.

Her brown eyes rose to meet his in protest. "Oh, yes, I do love you, Hal! It's just, not *that* way—" she finished lamely, feeling like a first-class heel.

"I don't care about that, Kathryn."

"What?"

"We'll work it out. Just let me take care of you, pamper you. The love will come later."

122

"Hal, do you know what you're saying?" Kaye was weak. First, his kiss. Now, this!

"I've never been more aware of anything in my life."

"Hal, I couldn't do . . . that!"

"Why? It would be perfectly legal. I'm asking you to marry me, Kathryn."

Her rubbery knees started to buckle and she sank to the leather sofa. "Hal . . . I can't!"

He was instantly beside her, cradling her hand. For a moment she feared that he would kneel before her. He didn't. In a hushed tone, he explained his proposal. "Kathryn, I will love you and take care of you . . . in style. You can live the way you want. And I will make no demands on you—none. Until you're ready."

Oh, God, he was serious! Her lips felt numb and her head whirled. "I . . . I don't know what to say. I have my life in Texas, Hal. And my business."

"To hell with your business! You can sell antiques here —or do whatever you want!" His voice had lost some of the gentleness, and frustration showed.

She twisted her hands together. "Hal, I . . ."

He stood and ran his hand around the back of his neck. "There's another man." It was a flat statement.

"Well, sort of. He's—"

Hal paced and held up his hand. "I don't want to hear about him. I don't want to know about your life in Texas —or your men."

Indignantly, she stood. "Men—Hal!"

He heaved a sigh. "I didn't mean that as it sounded, Kathryn. I . . . I'm sorry. I know I've hit you with a lot tonight. And I don't expect . . . no, I don't *want* an answer from you now. I want you to think about what I've said. About my offer. Living here, living with me, wouldn't be so bad, Kathryn. I would take very good care of you."

She wanted to scream, *I DON'T WANT ANYONE TO*

TAKE CARE OF ME! But something stopped her. Maybe it was her tears so frighteningly close to the edge.

"All you have to do is call me, Kathryn, and I will be here for you. Remember that." He wheeled and left her alone in the leather and wood-paneled den.

His words echoed against the empty walls long after he'd gone. Kaye stared morosely at the mementos of the past and wondered bleakly about her future. Was there a future for *them?* What about Matt?

Sunday was a disaster. No one mentioned it, but Kaye knew. Hal was uptight and formal. He wasn't at all like himself. Kaye had slept little the previous night . . . and looked it.

The time with old friends hung heavy over Kaye, and she couldn't understand it. She and Emery had enjoyed these friends, laughed with them, partied together. Somehow, they now seemed different. Their interests had changed.

As she slipped into Hal's Mercedes-Benz, she decided, with a jolt, *I've changed! It's me, not them!* She mulled over the revelation as she packed and gazed around the strange room in which she stood. Hal's room. Hal's house. Hal's life-style. Not hers. She didn't belong here anymore. She wasn't even Kathryn Coleman, widow of Emery Coleman. She was Kaye Coleman, her own person, and she belonged in Texas, where she could be accepted as such. It was a reassuring determination, filling her with pride and purpose.

Oh, yes, Matt, I'm coming home! Home, where I belong! Back to your arms, my darling! To our wonderful love!

The air was balmy when she deplaned at Dallas–Fort Worth Airport. Kaye shed her winter coat, and it was like removing a heavy cloak of the past. She was in Texas now.

124

She stepped off the ramp and into Matt's strong embrace. His kiss was fierce and wonderful, proclaiming his affection publicly to anyone who cared to notice.

She was home—in Matt's arms.

CHAPTER SEVEN

"Close your eyes!"

"Matt! Why?"

"Don't question my orders, woman! Just do it!" His voice was demanding, teasing, and his huge hands roughly directed her into the backyard. "Now, don't move, Kaye. Let me get the lights—and keep your eyes closed!"

She could hear Heidi's barking as Matt unlocked the back door. Immediately Heidi romped happily around Kaye's knees, and she groped blindly to pat the fluffy little dog. "Matt? What in the world are you up to?" Kaye found herself giggling. It was difficult to be dignified when standing with your eyes closed, waiting for—who knows what!

Matt's hands clasped around both her shoulders, guiding and pushing as Kaye stumbled with him through the grass. "Not yet! Come on over here."

Instinctively she pawed the air. "Where are you taking me? To the woods?"

"Not quite." He chuckled, halting her forward movement abruptly. "Okay! Now! You can open!"

Kaye stared, dumbfounded, at the surprise.

"Well," he encouraged her response. "How do you like it?"

Kaye was speechless and feared if she opened her mouth for any comment, she would break into tears. Matt's surprise was a newly constructed brick barbeque pit. There was nothing special about the thing, except that it reminded her so poignantly of the past life she was trying to forget.

Visions of the old brick structure that she and Emery had struggled to build back in Delaware raced through her tortured brain. The work, the laughter, the agony, the fun . . . "Oh, Matt, how could you?" Tears welled up in her eyes.

"Somehow, I thought you'd like it, Kaye." Matt looked at her strangely. This wasn't the reaction he had expected.

Her liquid brown eyes lifted to meet his. "Oh, I do like it." She wasn't very convincing.

Matt's steel-hard arm encircled her shoulders, and he pulled her close to his chest. A finger traced her cheekbone, wiping away the single tear. "Strange way to show your joy, Kaye. What's wrong?"

Her gaze swung back to the barbeque pit, and she reached out to touch a brick. "It's just that . . . Oh, Matt, I'm sorry. I can't let this happen every time something . . . something . . ." she faltered.

" . . . reminds you of Emery?" he finished.

Kaye nodded mutely, her hand still on the brick. Miserably, she thought, *Oh, God, is he angry? Probably. And he has every right to be. No man likes to be reminded of another man in his woman's life . . . even one who is no longer any competition.*

"Kaye, Kaye." Matt sighed her name huskily. "Come here to me, my pretty lady." In a surprising move, he reached down and picked her up, swinging her easily against his powerfully secure chest.

She grasped the muscles bracing his neck and buried her face there. His leathery fragrance engulfed her, and she breathed deeply, loving it. "Matt, oh, Matt!"

He nuzzled her ear. "We're going inside, and we're going to talk about some things, Kaye. And maybe . . . just maybe . . . we can put some of these old feelings to rest."

"Matt, I'm sorry I spoiled your surprise."

As he walked, he kissed her earlobe, her cheek, her neck. "You didn't spoil anything for me. I just don't understand you completely. But I intend to. We'll start tonight."

"You've already started understanding," she whispered. "Last week."

"Hmmm, and I liked what I learned," he murmured with a low laugh. "To me, sweetheart, your smile is worth a thousand tears. Someday, I hope there'll be a time when your smile will outlast the tears."

"Oh, Matt, you're so good to me. And patient." Kaye's hand touched his tanned cheek, turning his face to meet her waiting lips. Her kiss was impulsive as her featherlight tongue outlined his eager lips with soft teasing strokes. "I missed you," she murmured between soft caresses.

His response was serious. "I won't let you go alone again. I can't tell you how lifeless this place is without you. Without this—" And his mouth covered hers hungrily, meeting her gentle forays with his firm masculine demands. He paused long enough to open the door to the house and step inside with his lovely feminine cargo before kissing her again, kindling outbreaks of tiny fires deep within her. When he finally tore his lips away, Kaye clung weakly to his shoulders.

128

"Kaye, I cannot, *will not*, compete with Emery." The resolute sound of his voice jarred her. "What you had with him was obviously special, but, sweetheart, it's over. Face it. What we have is special, too. And it's different. Please, don't hang onto the past. I want you to enjoy the present, *now*. I want you to find pleasure in us."

"Matt"—her voice was a broken whisper—"I'm afraid I've put you in an unfair position."

He shook his head in protest. "I put myself in that position, Kaye."

She took a deep breath. "I don't compare you with him. I'm trying to forget everything about him. All the things we did, the way we lived, the people we knew, are behind me now—still in Delaware. It's just that we spent a whole summer building a barbeque pit. It was a disaster! Never worked right. But it looked like that one. Can you understand, Matt?"

"I'm trying to meet you halfway on this, Kaye."

She touched his face, tracing his jawline and across his mouth. "More than halfway. I love what we have together, Matt. It is very special."

He smiled and nuzzled her ear, holding her even closer to his chest. She could feel the rumbling of his words. "I'm glad to hear you say it. You resisted me for so long."

Her finger traced his straight nose and along his thin upper lip. "And see what I've missed?"

He laughed devilishly and walked toward the sofa, still carrying her. "I'll be glad to show you what you've missed!"

She kissed his neck and murmured, "You're right about us, Matt. What we have is special and good. You are very different from any man I've known. You're fun and good for me."

"I love to see that smile, Kaye."

She looked at the dark room, then back to Matt. "Are

129

you going to put me down, or are you just going to stand here and hold me all night?"

"I'm going to hold you all night, but not like this!"

"Is that a promise?" she asked, smiling wickedly.

"It's a promise!" Reluctantly he deposited Kaye on the sofa. "It's cool in here. I'll light a fire. Don't go away. I'll be right back." He whispered something in her ear, then left her blushing like a schoolgirl.

Kaye watched the muscles flex in Matt's broad back as he knelt before the fireplace. He was ruggedly athletic, appealing to her in a way that no man had before. Emery had been moderately athletic, leaning toward an occasional game of golf. But life with him had been somber and uneventful. Certainly the laughter hadn't flowed as readily as it did with Matt. Matt was really fun to be with. Was that so bad for her? *Fun,* after all these months?

He blew into the fireplace, scattering ashes everywhere.

Knowing that his efforts to build the outdoor grill were sincere, she thought she should patch up her earlier exhibition. "Matt, I really do like the brick grill. Now we can fix our steaks the way they should be done. But how in the world did you get it made so fast?"

A single flame licked upward, then blazed with a brilliant glow, giving a warm, flickering light to the room. Matt's large, masculine shape was outlined as he watched the fire momentarily. "Oh, I've been thinking about building it for a while. This weekend I just had the time."

"How could you have the time? I thought I left you with plenty to do. I happen to know your speaking schedule was full."

He leaned back on his haunches and watched the blaze take hold on a larger log. "Oh, there were a couple of hours on Saturday between the Ladies' Auxiliary lunch and the armadillo races and the chili cookoff. Today, I had only one event—the Polish kielbasa celebration. Ah, the

130

food was fantastic! Spicy, but great!" He rolled his eyes comically.

Kaye sympathized sarcastically. "Oh, the food politicians have to suffer through!"

He stood, rocked back on his heels, and hooked his thumbs through his belt loops and broke into his affected Texas drawl. "Folks out heah in Texas jes' figure it's a good way to meet oth-ah folks!" He tipped an imaginary hat and walked into the kitchen, leaving her rolling with laughter. She had forgotten Matt's fun-loving humor. Perhaps he was right . . . and she *had* forgotten how to laugh!

Matt busily clinked some glasses together. "Actually, I had some inner hostilities to work out, and the physical activity was good for me. You know, therapy with building blocks." He smiled wryly and shrugged. "Anyway, Davis came over today, and we made quick work of it."

"Inner hostilities?" Kaye stopped laughing and checked his face to see if he was serious. Sometimes it was hard to tell when he stepped over the line from the teasing. "What's wrong? Didn't the speeches go well? How's the campaign coming along?"

Matt's huge hands dwarfed the bottle of wine and two crystal glasses as he set them on the end table. "Oh, yes, my sassy little speech writer. The campaign is moving along just fine, except for the inevitable indigestion." He motioned with a fist to his midsection.

Kaye smiled apologetically as he poured the rosé. "Maybe I shouldn't have scheduled so many eating events in one day. I'm still learning how to do this, you know."

"Are *you* the one who arranged my schedule? Do you think my insides are made of steel?" He handed her the etched-crystal wineglass.

Her fingers clasped briefly around his as she accepted it. "Aren't you?" she asked innocently.

131

He flexed his bicep. "Just this. This is steel. But inside, I'm as fragile as this glass."

She stretched her hand around his rock-hard forearm. "Somehow, Matt, I always think of you as strong as steel all the way through."

"Not so, pretty lady." His shadowed face was close and the firelight flickered in his blue eyes. "When I couldn't reach you Friday night, then Saturday, then Saturday night, I turned to molten rock inside, worrying about you. I even called the airport to make sure your plane arrived safely."

"You worried about little ole' me?" she teased as her hand traveled across his muscular shoulder and into his hairline. It hadn't occurred to her that he would try to reach her.

He sat at her feet and rested his arm on her knees. After gulping the wine, he said, "You didn't check into the DuPont Hotel."

"Did you ever think I might be staying with friends?" She sipped her wine, hoping he wouldn't press her for an explanation.

He shrugged. "I assumed as much, when I couldn't find you."

Her fingers twirled the curly hair at the base of his neck. "I'm sorry you worried about me, Matt. I was with friends all weekend. Today there were ten of us gathered for brunch. And yesterday, Hal and I were busy all day at the auction. Oh, Matt, the auction was such fun! I bought some beautiful antiques for the shop."

"Where's the stuff now?"

Her answer was too quick, and she knew later she should have chosen her words more carefully. "Hal's going to hire someone to haul them across country. He is so good about taking care of everything."

"Who's Hal?" There was static in the air.

Kaye felt a tightness in her stomach. Why had she mentioned Hal's name again? She tried to make her tone casual, but each word mired her deeper. "Hal's just an old friend. He took care of the auction and helped me with . . . everything." She finished lamely.

"Is he married?"

She tried to shift and moved her hand from his shoulder. "No. He's divorced."

"Does he take good care of you, along with everything else?"

Indignantly, she stiffened. "Yes, as a matter of fact, he does! But not in the way you're insinuating!"

He was infuriatingly benign as he drawled, "And what way is that?"

"Matt!" Damn him! Not only did she set her own trap, but she was crawling into it step by step. And Matt just stood back smiling!

With slow deliberation, he reached for the wine bottle and refilled their glasses. Then, he settled against her knee again, his arm curling around her legs. A muscle in his cheek twitched as he demanded, "Who the hell is Hal? All this time, I thought I was fighting your husband's memory! Now I find that there's yet another man in your life!"

"Hal is not 'another man'! He is an old friend. I've known him for years. Our relationship is . . ." She paused, trying desperately to think of the right words to explain about Hal and his place in her life. Right now she wasn't very clear on that, herself. But she didn't want Matt to know.

"I know," Matt inserted sarcastically. "Your relationship is purely platonic!"

"Yes," she agreed quickly, nodding. "It is."

"Like hell!" he exploded. "Who could possibly spend that much time with you, Kaye, and not want you!"

Her eyes narrowed. "You're speaking from one point of

133

view!" Dear God! Is that what Hal wanted . . . *expected?* Deep inside, she knew the answer.

"I'm speaking from a man's point of view!"

"And a very jealous one, at that!"

His eyes narrowed. "You're damned right! I'm jealous as hell of anyone who looks at you, touches you, even an old friend who takes you to an auction!" Suddenly he was beside her on the sofa, his breath hot and sweet on her face. He buried his big hand underneath her hair and pulled her face close to his. "I'm not denying that charge at all. I know what I'm feeling for you, right now, my pretty lady. I want you, and I don't intend to share you with anyone—not even old friends!" His lips descended on hers with such fierce demand that she gasped for air and moaned with the painful pressure of his teeth on her tender lips. He kissed her hungrily, almost savagely, and Kaye found herself powerless in his grasp. He had never been so untamed and relentless with her as he was now; his hand roaming the sensitive areas of her neck and shoulders and breasts.

Kaye tried to protest, but found herself arching against his enticing touch. His hand slipped inside her blouse to capture her soft breast, snaring the tip and bringing it to quick prominence. She shuddered as waves of unrestrained passion washed over her, threatening to drown them both. Kaye's hand braced against Matt's chest, but instead of pushing him away, edged between the shirt buttons to dig into the soft mat of masculine hair. His flesh radiated warmth, and her own heated desires rose to match his.

The constant throbbing of her bruised lips reminded Kaye that she had to curtail Matt's force. She must alert him to his overpowering strength. Shoving against the muscular definition of his chest, she realized the futility of her act.

"Matt—" she moaned against her lips.

"Kaye, oh, Kaye, I want you!" He teased the corners of her mouth, soothing the tender lower edge, stroking her upper lip with his tongue. Her lips parted voluntarily, but the soft moan that escaped from her throat rose from a deeper instinct—one that she had refused to acknowledge until Matt entered her life. But now, with him, it seemed perfectly normal. So right! He was a man she could rely on, yet he made no demands, no commitments. He seemed to realize she wasn't ready for that now. Although Kaye denied love, or even devotion, to Matt, he excited her like no other man had. *Ever had? Was that possible? Even more than . . . oh, no!* She wouldn't let herself think that!

His kisses caressed her cheek and feverish temple. "Do you want me, Kaye?" he murmured against her earlobe.

The lusty boldness of his words titillated her. She licked her bruised lips and met his darkly passionate gaze. "You know I do."

His hand fumbled with the buttons on her blouse even before she answered. "That's what I've been waiting to hear for so long. Oh, Kaye, I want to love you!"

He left a path of hot, burning kisses from the unruly tendrils near her ear to the pulsating hollow of her throat, and on to the heated valley between her breasts. There was a pause before Kaye heard a frustrated oath, then the pop of stubborn buttons and ripping material.

"Damn little buttons!" He scowled, then muttered a quick apology while easily opening her bra.

"Take it easy, Matt. Can I help you?" She laughed with delight as he captured her creamy mounds with both hands.

He chuckled with relish. "No, thank you. I'll help myself!" And he did! His tongue was busy savoring, kneading, tasting the rounded tips until they rose to ripened perfection in his hands. Matt obviously took pleasure in caressing her breasts, her delicately molded curves. He seemed to cherish and to idolize her body, almost in a reverent manner. He was gentle now and moved with slow deliberation, making sure she, too, was enjoying the exquisite rhythm of his hands. He watched Kaye's eyes close in ecstasy and kissed them and her lips, and the rosy tips of her breasts. It was important to him that she respond to his touch. His own fulfillment carried less significance. Her relaxed passionate responses were his delight. "Kaye, do you like this? Talk to me."

She struggled for coherence. Matt demanded verbal approval, as well as physical response. Kaye had never— *never*, she could admit it now—felt such desires as Matt aroused in her. With the trails of fire that scorched her flesh at his touch, she could hardly *think*, much less *talk!*

"Kaye, can you hear me? Open your eyes!"

"Yes, yes, Matt," she murmured, her brown eyes opening enough to see his head bent to her breast. Firelight flickered a golden glow over them, and she reached for him, lacing her fingers through his blond hair. She could feel the heat emanating from him, igniting her own latent fires as she pressed him achingly closer. Her heart pounded uncontrollably against his lips as he dipped to the rigid peaks, taunting them repeatedly with his tantalizing tongue. She wondered if he could feel the vibrations as her heart hammered against the tender flesh he so skillfully excited. An inferno of desire mounted within Kaye, and her entire body quivered expectantly in his arms.

They still sat clumsily on the sofa, and Matt shifted. His hands slid to her ribs as he tried to pull her over him.

"Don't stop, Matt," she begged.

Matt knew he wanted much more of her than the narrow sofa allowed. And he wanted to give her the satisfaction she sought. His voice was thick as he instructed, "Take your clothes off for me, Kaye. Slowly. I want to see you. All of you." He pushed the blouse off her shoulders, and she realized that's what she wanted, too. *All of him!*

"Just a minute," she gasped. "Let me get up."

While she struggled clumsily with her clothing, Matt shed his shirt and shoes and socks. He sat, eyes glazed with passion, as she stood before him and dropped her blouse and bra atop his shirt. She turned away, but could feel his eyes on her as she undressed. With shaky hands, she scooted the skirt over her hips. Only panty hose remained, and she bent once again to discard them. Then, with inner trepidation, Kaye stood before him. She hoped he couldn't see her trembling, nor tell that her heart pounded in her throat so hard that she thought she would choke.

Her slight shudder did not go unnoticed, and his groan of anticipation was barely audible. The fire flared to reveal the palest apricot tanned shoulders and the white curve of her full breasts, branded with alert, roseate tips. His hands cupped them both, while his mouth paid silent tribute to the skin of her abdomen.

Then he stepped back, but was still close enough for his masculine fragrance to engulf her, filling her with heady desire. She heard the unmistakable slide of his zipper and kept her eyes on his face.

"Look at me, Kaye. Don't be ashamed. I know you want to."

She felt her face burn at his bold suggestion. "Matt! I—" She was about to protest, but he took her hand.

"Kaye, I think your body is beautiful. I'd like to think you feel the same about me."

"Oh, Matt, I do." Obediently her eyes traveled from his familiar, square-jawed face down his corded neck to the muscles that graced his chest and ribs. She had rested her head on those muscles and cried on them, but had not relished their golden-tanned glory. She ran her fingers through the sandy hair that grew in the middle of those rounded muscles and down to his waist, and beyond. When her eyes reached the part of him that was natural and untanned, she swayed uncertainly. With an embarrassed smile, she gazed into his eyes. "You have a very nice body, Matt."

His hands reached to support her, caressing her smooth shoulders and arms, delicately capturing her firm buttocks. He lingered there, feeling her body tensing with the passion that hungered to be released. Then his hands moved up to her slim waist, encircling it. Gently nudging her closer to him, his palms wandered down the silken curves of her hips. He pulled her hips to meet his. "Kaye, Kaye, this is so beautiful. Don't be ashamed of what is happening to us."

With a shaky sigh, she slid her hands over his chest, lingering over the muscle conformation, the feathery hair, the taut male nipples. "I'm not ashamed, Matt. I'm just learning to love again."

His voice was gentle. "Are you nervous this time?"

She tossed her head and smiled. "No. Anticipating!"

"Oh, God, me too!" Matt's lips claimed hers fiercely, and she responded to his warm, probing desires. She opened her lips eagerly to his thrusting tongue, inviting his penetration of her sweetness. Her hands climbed the powerful wall of his chest until they entwined in the golden hair that curled at the base of his neck. Her enthusiastic touch inflamed him even more, and he molded her slim, soft body to his hard, demanding force. Kaye moaned softly as she felt him against her, knowing their desires would soon be satisfied. She felt deliciously giddy and weak with the torrents of passion that coursed through her veins, threatening to topple her. Just as she thought she could stand with him no longer, his strong hands guided

138

her. They lowered, as one, to the sensuous white fur beneath their bare feet.

Hovering over her trembling body, Matt cradled her head in his hands, tucking a stray wisp of hair away from her half-closed eyes. "Oh, Kaye, I want to love you . . . want you completely." His mouth possessed her lips while his hands danced erotically down the length of her silken form, stroking the smooth curve of her hip, the soft flatness of her abdomen, the warm flesh of her inner thigh, until Kaye thought she would faint from the overwhelming pleasure of his touch.

As he knelt over her, she let her eyes devour his masculine perfection. Then, she closed her eyes as her fingers delicately traced hot designs of passion over Matt's broad chest and darted around to tease the smooth planes of his back in gradually bolder strokes. Sighing with contentment, she moved her palms down to massage the curve of his buttocks, then let her trembling hands travel to newly discovered territory, rejoicing in the solidly muscled flesh that hovered so enticingly near. She reached up to grab his waist in a bear hug that quickly brought him down to her waiting arms. The ecstasy that engulfed them was all-encompassing, leaving Kaye and Matt completely sated. Kaye had expected such vigor from Matt, but was surprised by her own ardent passion.

These wonderful moments with Matt were times of total freedom and complete joy. No guilt. No sadness. Not even any remembering. Just ecstasy.

Lying quiet and still beneath him, Kaye knew the satisfaction of complete fulfillment in Matt's embrace. She was filled with such happiness, she wanted to sing . . . or shout with joy. Kaye felt like a new woman, grateful to Matt for being so persistent and loving. Yes, loving. She was, at that moment, completely fulfilled. And loved. And it was a wonderful feeling.

She moved her hands down his back from where she had tightly gripped his shoulders, to the narrowing of his waist, and firm-muscled hips. The contrast of this brawny male against her and the soft rug that cushioned her was definitely erotic. Matt had been right. The only way to truly enjoy this New Mexican sheepskin was nude!

Their warm bodies emitted a pleasant fragrance of mingled leather and exotic foreign flowers. Their blending was lusty and wild; unlikely, yet expected. She was soft, delicate, refined. He was hard, gregarious, aggressive. Was it too much to expect their pairing to be fulfilling, or lasting? Or was she just attracted to Matt because of his virility? Perhaps she savored their sexual conquest because of his contrast to her! She couldn't refute the notion that Matt simply aroused her baser instincts of unfulfilled lust.

Was she just a challenge for this athletic hero who could have any woman he desired? Was that challenge now met? Would this wonderful love of theirs end quickly? She squeezed her eyes shut in anguish. Whatever made her think that? After all, he had declared that he didn't want to lose her; had vowed to keep her close. Couldn't she believe him? Shouldn't she?

The fire crackled loudly and she raised her eyes to him, realizing only then that Matt was studying her face. "What are you thinking, pretty lady?" He kissed her wrinkled brow until it smoothed.

She smiled up at him. "Oh, just how wonderful I'm feeling right now with you."

"Then, why the frown?" He settled next to her on the rug, offering his arm as a pillow.

"I don't want this to ever end, Matt. It's too wonderful." Suddenly, she felt very emotional.

His arms enfolded her securely and his voice was low. "This isn't the end, my pretty lady. It's just the beginning for us."

She snuggled against him, assured by his convincing words, safe in his strong arms. "Did I tell you how much I missed you this weekend?"

His voice vibrated through her, and she felt his words, rather than heard them. "How could you, when you were so busy? Going here with Hal, going there with Hal. It's a wonder you didn't bring him back with you!"

She smiled at the thought. "Now what in the world would we have done with Hal tonight if I had brought him back with me?"

He nuzzled her ear. "I know what *I* would do with him! Hal, or anyone else who interferes with us, goes the way of the dog—OUT!"

She giggled and drew a line down his rib cage with her fingernail. "Oh no! Not Hal Kamerman III! People chauffeur him to airports just to have an audience with him and plead for his inclusion on their business deals!"

His hand slid over her silky skin to cup her soft breast. "I can assure you that I don't want the man's inclusion in my business! You are my business, Kaye, and I don't want him near you!"

"Now, Matt. He's just a dear, old friend," she placated.

Suddenly he was serious. "Tell me about this 'dear, old friend.' Did you spend the weekend with him?"

Why couldn't she just lie to him and end this now? She cleared a catch in her throat before answering. "Yes, but—"

He interrupted and his tone was unduly hard. "Yes, but—he didn't touch you?"

She chattered rapidly before thinking of an answer. "Hal has a very large house, Matt! And he just insisted that I stay there. Anyway, his housekeeper and her husband were there." The fact that she never saw them would remain untold.

He propped himself up beside her, his warm hand sliding to her waist. "What has the size of the house got to do with the question? Did he touch you?"

Indignation rose hotly within her. Damn him! He had a way of finding out whatever he wanted to know. If only she could lie to him! She looked into his serious blue eyes and knew she couldn't! "Matt—" she began gently.

"So, he did!" he exploded, finishing her lame reply.

"No—yes, but nothing—"

"He didn't take you to bed?"

"Matt, please!" Kaye sat up, rubbing her forearm nervously. "No, we didn't go to bed together! Are you satisfied?"

He paused for a moment, trying to assess the situation and understand why she was so upset. "How long have you known him?"

She took a deep, shaky breath. "Hal and Emery were friends even before we married. He was our lawyer and business adviser for years."

"Is he your business adviser now? Did he advise you to come to Texas?" His voice was gentle for he was beginning to comprehend more than Kaye was willing to tell. Perhaps more than she was willing to admit to herself.

She smiled at the suggestion. "Oh, heavens no! He had a fit when I decided to come out here! His fondest wish would be for me to move back to Delaware!"

He touched her shoulder. "Did he try to get you to stay this time?"

"Yes."

The singular sound of the fire seemed to hang in the air. "Why didn't you?"

Her hands grasped his face fiercely. *Damn you, anyway, Matt Logan! If you don't know by now!* "Because my life . . . and love . . . is here in Texas!"

He stared at her liquid brown eyes, as if not believing

142

what she was saying. Finally, he mumbled thickly, "Oh, Kaye . . . kiss me! Love me . . . love me again!"

She kissed him with so much fervor, and cradled his head against her with such tenderness, and caressed him with such passionate strokes that he believed in love again. And so did she. As the fire's embers smoldered, they stumbled together to her bed and slept, curled together, contented and fulfilled.

CHAPTER EIGHT

Nan's face beamed with her excitement. "Oh, Kaye, look! More flowers!" She hurried the length of the shop carrying a long green florist's box. "And something tells me these are special!"

Kaye straightened up from where she was bent, rubbing up the magnificent wood luster of a shell-designed, mahogany high chest. "Who are they from?"

"I don't know, but if you'll hurry up and open them, we'll find out!" Nan urged excitedly.

The shop's windows were already full of potted plants. Kaye's grand opening had attracted numerous well-wishers. Even the mayor, Gil Ashland, had sent an arrangement of gorgeous yellow mums, much to Matt's chagrin.

"Someone special, huh?" Matt joined Kaye, his hand resting casually, but possessively, on her shoulder.

Kaye smiled knowingly at him before tearing off the ribbon. She opened the long box as the four of them leaned to look inside. There, carefully wrapped in tissue paper, were a dozen long-stemmed, burgundy roses.

144

Nan, who was usually more reserved, squealed with delight. "Oh, they're beautiful! See who sent them!"

Kaye's eyes sparkled as she gazed first at the flowers, then at Matt's stiff countenance. She inhaled the sweet essence before lifting the small white card nestled among the glorious blooms. She stared silently. Matt read the card aloud from over her shoulder.

> *Kathryn,*
> *All my wishes are for your success and happiness.*
>> *Love,*
>> *Hal*

Kaye blinked at the card, then at the roses. She was as startled to see Hal's name on the card as anyone. She had fully expected that the roses were a gift from Matt.

"Hal?" It was Nan who asked. "Who's Hal?"

"He's . . ." began Kaye lamely. "Hal's an old friend from Delaware."

"Sounds like a very good friend, too," Matt growled. "How thoughtful of him, Kaye. I'm sure he wishes he were here in person to offer his wishes for success! To hell with his wishes!"

"Hell, Matt, you'd better be glad Hal's not here!" Davis laughed and clapped his buddy on the back.

"Well, I think they're beautiful, Kaye. You're very lucky to have someone who cares so much about you," Nan defended her friend.

Matt squeezed Kaye's arm affectionately. "And I'm damn glad he's not here to congratulate you in person! Now, get rid of the damn things!"

"He's right. We'd better find a vase for these beautiful roses before they wilt from all the hot air in this room!" Nan steered Kaye to the back room.

Davis looked curiously at Matt. "Who the hell is that dude, Matt? Does he mean anything to her?"

Matt shrugged. "She says he doesn't. He has been a family friend for years. But, during the past year, he's hovered especially close to her."

Davis sighed. "Sometimes old friends are the worst kind. Obviously, he does care about her."

"Yeah," agreed Matt, a worried grimace on his face.

Davis slapped his knee and smiled. "Well, like I said, just be grateful that this Hal is two thousand miles away!"

Matt nodded. "That, and there's only one more week of this campaign until the election."

"Are you ready for the last big push? I think you have some personal appearances every day. Nan has that schedule. This is it! And we're gonna give it our best shot!"

"Uh, Davis," Matt began hesitantly. "You know when we went into this damn-fool thing, we agreed that my chances of winning were slim and none."

"Yep. But that's changed now." Davis grinned confidently.

"No it hasn't. They're still slim, and you know it."

"Listen, buddy," Davis rumbled, propping his booted foot on a black, cast-iron stove. "If you're trying to tell me you're gonna lose, I'm not listening. This thing we started has gone too far, and we've worked too hard to even consider it. Now, you get your ass in gear for this last week! Then, you get ready to move into the mayor's office!"

Matt stuffed his hands into his jeans' pockets. "But, Davis—"

Davis raised his mitt of a hand and reached for his jacket. "I told you. Get ready! Now, is this all the furniture you need me to move? We've got to be going. I have to pick up the boys from football practice and feed the cattle." He called to the storage room: "Nan, are you ready to go?"

Matt mumbled, "Thanks for everything."

Nan approached with a smile, followed by Kaye who carried the tall vase of roses. "Aren't they just beautiful? Oh, Kaye, the shop looks fantastic! I can hardly wait until tomorrow's opening!"

Catching the disgruntled look in Matt's eyes, she placed the roses in an obscure spot. "Yes, and I never could have done all this without your help. Thanks, Davis, for hauling all this heavy furniture. And, Nan, your assistance has been invaluable! We're going to work great together." She hugged them both.

Matt and Davis shook hands, their eyes meeting to exchange mixed messages.

"Tomorrow at ten!" And they were gone, leaving Matt and Kaye alone in an uneasy silence.

Kaye busied herself rearranging flowers, for the fourteenth time that day.

Matt straightened one corner of a highboy, then gathered the padding blankets they had used. He brushed by the flowers and a primitive urge rose in him to heave the damn things against the wall. But he kept going. He knew Hal was a dominant figure in Kaye's past. And, apparently, he wanted to be a part of her future. It was obvious that the man cared for her. Most importantly, what were Kaye's feelings for Hal?

Matt glanced around. "Are you ready to go, Kaye? I think Ye Olde Antique Shoppe is ready for tomorrow's ribbon-cutting, don't you?"

Kaye nodded, an unavoidable smile spreading across her face. "I just can't believe it! This is a dream come true, Matt, and I'm so excited! My own business!"

"I know, baby! Believe it! Because tomorrow, the doors

147

swing open! How about dinner in the big city tonight? You deserve a celebration. We'll go someplace special."

"I'd love to, Matt." There was a happy glow about her face, and Matt was drawn to her magnetic allure.

His lips captured hers, lingering with feathery whispers. "So proud . . . beautiful smile . . . love you . . . gift, my pretty lady . . ." He was pressing something into her hand.

Kaye's eyes flew open, and she looked down at the small white box in her hand. A sharp gasp escaped when she saw the name James Avery embossed in gold in one corner. The name was synonymous with beautifully crafted gold jewelry. "Oh, Matt . . . you shouldn't!"

"Well, open it. You don't know if I should have or not," he encouraged gruffly.

With shaky hands she lifted the lid and gazed inside the tiny box. "Oh, Matt! It's perfect!" Nestled in purple velvet lay an exquisite golden necklace. It was a miniature replica of the scroll-shaped sign that hung outside her shop. On it, the words Ye Olde Antique Shoppe were inscribed in Old English lettering. She turned it over where Love, Matt was etched. Tears of happiness filled Kaye's large brown eyes as she met his proud gaze. "Oh, Matt, it's absolutely beautiful. You had it made especially for me!"

His arms swept around her. "You are very special to me, Kaye. When are you going to realize that?" His lips sought hers in a tender, sensuous proclamation of his affection.

"I think I'm beginning to get the message," she whispered. "And I love it."

"Hmmm, good. Come on, Kaye, I want to take you home *now!*" He nibbled urgently at her earlobe and neck.

"Matt, please, someone will see us." She pushed gently on his chest. "I love the necklace. Thank you." She fingered the design, then lifted it for Matt to attach around her neck.

He took the delicate object in his large hands and struggled at the clasp while she lifted her hair. "I know how hard you've worked to get this shop going, Kaye. And I figured you'd like a remembrance of your first business. There! How does it look?"

"My first business? You make it sound like there will be more." She peeked into a nearby antique mirror, smiling with satisfaction at the reflection.

"Sure, there'll be more! I figure that within a few years you'll have a chain of Ye Olde Antique Shoppes around the country!"

"A chain of antique shops?" The idea was mind-boggling to a person who had yet to open her first business. But she smiled thoughtfully at the prospect. "Matt, your help and encouragement have been tremendous. I appreciate you so much!"

He spread his big hands in a shrug. "I want to see you succeed. And you will."

"Matt, do you realize . . . *really realize* how much this business means to me? Your suggestion of a chain of stores sounds challenging, but not impossible. Not now! Two years ago, even a year ago, it would have been unthinkable."

"Sweetheart, nothing's impossible for you!"

Her voice was low and honest. "That's easy for you to say. But, Matt, this shop is the first thing I've ever done on my own. It was my dream, my idea, my creation. I'm proud of that."

"And you should be. I'm proud of you, too. Always remember, I'll do anything I can to help you. Anything to make you happy." He steered her toward the door.

"I am happy with you, Matt." She slipped her arms into the jacket he held for her, then turned to him. "I want you to know that I think the roses from Hal are lovely, but he doesn't really understand me or the needs I have in my life

149

now. He wants me to be happy, but under his terms, not mine. Thank you, Matt, for letting me be me."

With a sigh of relief, he kissed her spontaneously. When he raised his head, he teased, "It's about time, pretty lady. Let's go home, and you'll appreciate me even more!"

"Oh, you!" She tweaked his nose with a giggle. "And you keep me laughing, Matt Logan! I like that!"

He locked the door to the shop, and they walked down the street, arm-in-arm. Tomorrow her new business would open, and another facet of her life would begin. But she wasn't alone anymore. It was a nice feeling.

CHAPTER NINE

It was one of those election days that politicians hate. Rain; not heavy, just a constant drizzle all day. And a cold November rain, at that.

Matt figured that rain on election day either worked for or against the candidate, but it was never the same as if it hadn't rained. And the determination wasn't made until later, after the talleys. Then someone decided, "Oh, you lost because your constituents stayed home and didn't want to get wet"; or "You won because your opponent's supporters couldn't cross the flooded-out bridge." Matt reckoned, even before the vote, that the rain would work against him.

However, until the seven o'clock closing of the polls, he stood in the doorways of schools and shook hands in the cold drizzle, hoping to get that last-minute edge.

Oh, they all came over to shake hands and talk. They wanted to touch him and say, "I saw you when you hurt your knee playing the Cowboys in the rain!" Or, "I was in Denver when you recovered the fumble to score against the Broncs, and it was three below!" Matt couldn't be sure how they would vote, but they remembered his pro-football career with gusto. However, would they trust their city government to a man who had played in ball games as a career? Time would answer that question soon enough, Matt thought wearily as he drove into the Chandler's driveway. A small crowd had already gathered there to await the election returns.

Matt squinted through the darkness and mist. Damn! Kaye's little blue sports car was not among them. He had not seen her all day, and he missed her like hell. She had insisted on working at the shop, claiming that he would make a better impression with the town's voters without her. Maybe she was right, politically. She always was. He only knew that he wanted her near him. *So, where the hell is she now?*

He sighed heavily and opened the car door. She would be here soon enough. After all, this was her election, too. He had drawn her into it, and she had done a helluva good job for him. And he loved her for it.

"Matt! Come on in. We've been waiting for you. Oh, you look tired." Nan's arms reached up to hug his broad shoulders. "You're wet! Even your shirt's damp! Come with me. We'll find some dry clothes. I'm sure Davis has a shirt that'll fit you." She led him quickly down the hall to the back of the house before the small crowd could spot him.

"Is Kaye here?" he mumbled, knowing the answer.

"No. But she'll be here soon, I'm sure. She worked until five, y'know."

"Yeah. She just had to keep that shop open today." There was a touch of resentment in his tone.

Nan opened Davis's closet door and began sorting through the shirts. "I think Kaye felt she had to keep busy today. She's not the type to stand around and worry. And,

152

that's exactly what she would have done if she hadn't opened the shop."

"Yeah. I guess." Matt was unbuttoning his rain-dampened shirt.

"Here, muscle-boy. See if this one fits. It'll match your baby-blues when they snap your winning picture! Come on out when you're ready, and I'll have an ice-cold Coors waiting for you." Nan smiled reassuringly and slipped through the door.

Another hour passed before Kaye finally arrived. And, oh, God, she looked ravishing! As she shed her waist-length fur jacket, her mahogany eyes scanned the crowd. She had abandoned the Texas look with her prairie dresses and ruffled blouses. Tonight, her style was casually elegant, and classy—very Eastern. Tawny hair touched the shoulders of her winter-white sweater. The flattering V-neckline was edged with taupe piping that nearly matched her hair. The cream-colored wool slacks emphasized her long, straight legs and slim hips. Her searching eyes met Matt's across the room and an implied message was exchanged. With twenty-five people watching, they could do nothing more than smile and nod . . . and promise silently.

Matt continued to circulate through the crowd, which, by now, was quite large. He knew it was important to spend time with the people who lent their time, money, and support to a stranger who dared to oppose Gil Ashland's political machine. But *she* was important to him, too. He had to be alone with Kaye, if only for a few moments.

She clutched the cup of hot tea, nervously chatting with Nan about how slow the business had been today. As Matt moved past her, his hand rested casually on Kaye's shoulder. He leaned close to murmur in her ear, "Five minutes, back porch." There was an urgency in his tone and touch that did not go unnoticed.

Minutes later, Matt hunched his shoulders against the stinging wind. The rain had stopped, and a damp coldness hung in the air. Kaye slipped quietly through the back door and into his open embrace. Her arms encircled his rib cage, absorbing the warmth she found there.

His huge body shuddered around her in a bear hug, drawing strength from her slight, strong body, burying his face in the warm hollow of her neck. They stood like that for long minutes, clinging to each other, communicating what no words could ever say.

Finally, as he inhaled her exotic fragrance, Matt muttered, "God, it's been a long day without you."

"Election days are always long. How are you? You look tired." She gazed up at him, keeping her arms around his chest.

He sighed. "I'm beat. And I missed you today, pretty lady. Oh, God, do I need you!" His lips covered hers in a tender acclamation of his words, lingering, caressing, drawing from her sweetness.

"And I thought you'd be too busy to notice I wasn't there today."

His hand stroked her back. "Never too busy for you, Kaye. It was a hellish day. You were right to stay in the shop. The rain was very cold."

She laughed softly. "I should have closed at noon. I don't think I pulled in fifty dollars. But I stayed busy."

"Kaye, if, uh, you know the weather wasn't the best for a newcomer on the political scene in this town," Matt began, obviously paving the way for something. "Rain usually favors the incumbent."

"Rain is equally bad for both," Kaye protested.

He shook his head. "I . . . I don't think we can expect to do very well."

"Now, Matt, that's the wrong attitude. We are going to win! You will be the next mayor! Isn't it exciting?"

"Kaye, you know what I'm trying to tell you!"

"And I won't listen. I didn't work my butt off this last month to see you lose! And neither did you! You are going to do just fine!"

"But, Kaye, there's a good chance—"

She placed her fingers over his lips, outlining the top briefly with her index finger. "No, there is not a chance of your losing. And I won't even consider it!"

The door opened and Nan's excited voice penetrated the damp darkness. "Hey, Matt! The first precinct just called in! You're ahead by ten votes!"

"See?" whispered Kaye triumphantly. She stood on tiptoe and kissed him quickly, then turned happily to Nan, leading Matt by the hand as far as the door.

"Ten votes," he groaned half-aloud, knowing that lead was insignificant.

Premature congratulations were loud and boisterous as they entered the room again. The crowd was growing and everyone wanted to touch and talk with the candidate. As the evening wore on, additional calls from various precincts added to the agitation. The tally was neck and neck. Counts were low, and when Matt led in one precinct, Gil led in another.

Finally, the tension was almost unbearable as they waited for the final two precincts to report in. Voices grew loud and shrill. The ranch house took on a carnival atmosphere and you could catch such words as *celebration* and *unbelievable* and *overthrow the machine*. You could feel the excitement in the air.

Yet, through it all, Matt contained himself. He knew, perhaps he just felt, his chances were slim. He had tried to warn Kaye so the disappointment wouldn't be so acute. Stubbornly, she wouldn't listen. They all wanted a winner, including Kaye.

Another phone call. The crowd quieted immediately

while Davis took the numbers. Stoically, he turned a somber face to the anxious crowd. "Ashland, 489. Logan, 454. He's ahead by 35."

A murmur rolled through the crowd; disappointment hung in the air. Then someone spoke aloud about "expectation" and "hopeful until the last vote is in," and everyone began talking at once. The final call came around eleven thirty. Kaye held her breath, knowing from Davis's stricken expression that Matt had lost.

"Ashland continues as mayor by a majority of 58 votes! Fifty-eight goddamn, miserable votes! Damn! Sorry, folks, but—" Davis threw up his hands in dismay. His expletives embodied everyone's anger and disappointment and pain. Of course, there would be recounts, but they knew . . . it was over!

Tears stung Kaye's eyes as reality sunk in. Matt stood on one step of a kitchen stool and raised his hand to quiet the crowd. They listened, some with tears streaming down their faces, some with stunned expressions, others exhibiting anger at what they had feared . . . and fought.

Matt's voice was strong. "Ladies and gentlemen, friends, I want to thank you, my loyal supporters, for all the help in this campaign. It is not the end for Twin Oaks. It is a new beginning. We have worked very hard, fought a good battle, but most importantly, we have planted a seed. And I firmly believe that seed will grow. Don't let it die! It's up to you!" Matt's blue eyes seemed bluer, matching his borrowed shirt, as he stepped down, and the photographer from the local newspaper snapped what would be the losing picture. Everyone applauded and began talking and reaching for him. There were last-minute things to be said to this man who came into their small community and stood up for them and some ideals they had let slide. It was their own fault. Now it was up to them to make future changes.

There were hugs and handshakes and private pledges to exchange—it won't happen again—and a phone call to the winner, conceding the victory. Kaye moved through the crowd, responding, listening, comforting. It was almost like a dream, more like a nightmare. Finally, the crowd began thinning. Someone popped corks from a couple of champagne bottles and began to pour small amounts into Styrofoam cups. Davis, who was the most disappointed, proposed a toast. "A salute to my friend, Matt Logan, who fought one helluva battle . . . for us. Thanks, Matt!"

The applause was loud and Matt smiled and held up his hand for attention. "I'd like to toast my staff: Davis, who managed all the funds; Nan, who kept everything moving forward, and Kaye, my manager and the most expensive speech writer we could afford!" At the end everyone applauded and smiled through their tears.

Matt gulped his small allotment of champagne, then reached for Kaye's hand. "Let's get out of here." Quickly, they bid everyone good night and walked out into the misty Texas night, arm-in-arm.

As they stepped into her dark den, the impact of the evening seemed to settle heavily around Kaye. She turned to him with large, liquid eyes. "Oh, Matt, I can't believe you lost!" Her arms wrapped around him fiercely, and she cried at last, burying her tearstained face against his rock-hard chest.

As on a previous occasion, Matt allowed her tears to flow, giving the physical support of his strong arms about her, encompassing her with his love. When, finally, she lifted her chin, he kissed away the tears and murmured sweet words she longed to hear . . . needed to know . . . cried for. "Hey, pretty lady, you're ruining those beautiful brown eyes. I can't even see them for all this water! This isn't the end. Don't take it so hard. There'll be other times, other campaigns. I knew you'd be disappointed. That's why I tried to warn you."

With great effort, she smiled through her tears. "Yes, you did. But I wouldn't listen. I just couldn't imagine them not choosing you," she admitted, and shuddered against him again.

"You're cold, Kaye. Let go, and I'll start the fire. Then I'll warm you up."

She grinned at his mild attempt at humor, even now. "Okay. And I have something for you."

"Hope so!" He chuckled and lifted her up to kiss her nose.

She laughed and grabbed playfully at him. "It's champagne, smart aleck! It was meant for our own private celebration. We'll celebrate, anyway."

He set her down and nuzzled her earlobe, sending warm tingles over her. "We'll toast each other!"

Later, Kaye and Matt curled together on the sofa in front of the blazing fire. Wrapped in the warmth of each other's arms, sipping champagne, luxuriating in the sweet wine of an occasional kiss, the political battle seemed far away. The challenge, the opportunity, the hard work, the disappointment were all finished . . . over . . . behind them. They needed time to unwind and know complete acceptance to counter the awful feeling of rejection that came with losing the election. Perhaps the champagne would help them do that.

Another thought haunted them tonight, although they held it back. There was the inevitable question of what all this would do to their relationship. One thing was assured: it would change.

At last, Kaye whispered it. "Matt, what will happen to us?"

Matt rested his cheek against hers. "Nothing. Nothing will happen to us, sweetheart. We'll always be the same."

It was a lie and they both knew it. His lips sealed hers tightly, and they both believed the lie because they wanted to . . . needed to . . . right then.

The bottle of champagne was half gone when Kaye hit upon the perfect way to forget the campaign. Maybe it was the wine, maybe the events of the evening, maybe it was a desperate effort to hold onto the man she loved that influenced her behavior. In fact, she hadn't even admitted to herself that she loved him. She only knew she didn't want to lose him. She wanted to make him stay with her, even if she had to entice him.

Kaye squirmed out of Matt's arms and stood before him, her curves outlined by the fire's glow. She leaned over and kissed him, whispering against his lips, "Follow me! The night is young, and so are we!" She wheeled around, grabbed the champagne bottle by its neck, and swished out.

"My God! What an invitation!" Matt exclaimed, struggling to his feet.

By the time he reached the doorway to her bedroom, an easy-listening FM radio station crooned soft background music and a small lamp cast gentle shadows on the bed.

Kaye pulled him into the room, kissing him, while at the same time unbuttoning his borrowed blue shirt. When the last button allowed the shirt to fall open, she ran her hands up his bare torso, pausing to circle fingers in the mat of blond hair on his chest.

Matt's hands curved naturally around her shoulders. "Hey, pretty lady, have you gone crazy?"

"Crazy?" she laughed. "Yes, I suppose you could say that!"

"I love it, but—"

Her hands reached his shoulders and began easing his shirt off. "If you love it, then be quiet. Let me see if I can do this!"

"Do what?" His arms hugged her, lifting her up and taking them both in a merry circle.

"Put me down, Matt!" she shrieked in exasperation. "You damned macho male! Let me make love to you, for a change!"

"Okay, okay!" He laughingly set her on her feet. "I didn't mean to spoil your party, my wicked little female!"

"Wicked, huh?" She grasped his belt and unzipped his trousers, letting them fall around his ankles. He kicked them into the pile with his shirt. In another moment, his briefs were off and she scraped her fingers enticingly over him, stroking, driving him wild.

"Kaye—"

"Now comes the good part!" She turned him around and pushed him toward the bed. "I want you there!"

"Hey, that's my line!" He teased, but obliged by stretching his nude masculine frame the length of her massive antique oak bed.

"Exactly!" she beamed. She took the champagne bottle and turned it up for a big gulp, as if she needed its fortification in order to continue. She turned her back to him and inched the sweater over her head, slowly, ever so slowly. Tossing the garment casually into the corner, she pivoted to face him again to reveal creamy breasts cupped in ecru lace. The pink-brown wreathes at the tips peeked tantalizingly through the thin material, straining to be free. And, oh, God, Matt wanted to liberate them! But the sensuous mood was set in motion, and he dared not disrupt it.

With thumbs hooked under the waistband of her ivory slacks, Kaye nudged them off her hips in short jerky impulses. She rotated with her swaying body only a hand's reach away from Matt and kicked her feet free of the slacks. This time she faced him tantalizingly with only her flimsy bra and brief lace-edged panties covering the parts of her that he wanted most.

160

Music filled the background and the vague harmony of "The Taste of Honey" inspired Kaye to sing along softly. Her hands molded to her curves, erotically emphasizing what Matt longed to touch and taste. His hazy blue eyes revealed a certain agony of having to hold back. He was so accustomed to being the aggressor, especially with Kaye, that he grappled with the anguish of this new passive role. But he definitely found it stimulating. He locked his hands behind his head, as if to enjoy the scene before him. However, it was as much to clinch his hands tightly as anything!

The records switched to bossa nova, and Kaye used its sensuous beat to complete her task. She ran her forefingers deep into the scanty briefs and all around the front edge, while the sway of her hips kept time with the music. Then her hands traveled gracefully up her rib cage to the confinement of her bra. She unsnapped the front opening, then began the agonizingly slow process of easing it off. Eventually, she flipped it away and those pert strawberry tips danced maddeningly before Matt's eyes.

Matt licked his lips in anticipation of touching and tasting those tender morsels. His eyes glazed with passion as he watched her reach down. In a seemingly endless effort, she rolled the beige panties with her palms until they were a narrow strip crossing the top of her legs and not quite hiding the light reddish-brown tuft at the juncture.

Kaye cast a quick, satisfied glance at Matt's aroused masculine form as she worked with that stubborn roll of silky cloth. Her brown eyes met his steadily and she knew that she had accomplished her goal. She had mesmerized him so completely that now and for the moments to follow, he couldn't possibly be thinking about the election, the loss, or even the future. He could only dwell on immediate delights. And her actions assured him there were plenty.

She smiled with great pleasure and raised first one leg, then the other, to eliminate the scrap of cloth that hid her complete feminine form from his view. She swayed and danced closer and closer, as the bossa nova beat reached its finale. With the abrupt musical ending, she, too, was finished.

She stood proudly before him, then before he could catch his breath, she bent over to kiss him, allowing her breasts to feather their tips on his heaving chest.

"My God, Kaye! That was beautiful! You're fantastic!" He unclasped his hands and reached for her.

"Not yet!" she admonished, as his hands raked down her shimmering body. She raised the champagne bottle to her pink lips for another sip. Then she tipped the bottle toward his lips. "Want some?"

He nodded and raised upon one elbow to take it. But she continued to hold it while he drank. A little of the liquid dribbled down his chin. "Easy, Kaye, you'll spill—"

But she shoved his shoulder flat against the bed.

"What the—"

With a sassy grin, Kaye tilted the bottle devilishly. A tiny bubbly stream trickled from his neck, into the curly haired valley between rounded chest muscles, along the flat, narrow trail to his sunken navel.

"My pretty lady has turned into a devil-woman to-night!" He whooped, laughing at her dirty tricks.

Her smile was glorious as she counseled, "Never mind, Matt. I'll clean it up." And she knelt beside him on the bed and began to lap the moist trail that led down his body. Her wicked darting tongue lit a flame of hot desire over his chest and navel, all the way to his inner thigh.

"Oh, Kaye," he groaned, his hands stroking her back and buttocks.

"Do you like that? Talk to me, Matt." She giggled, reminding him of his previous demands on her to talk in the midst of passion's grip.

He buried his hands in her hair. "You're driving me crazy, devil-woman! Come here!"

"Not yet . . ." she teased, her hands playing across his body.

"Now! Yes, now!" he rasped, tugging her roughly across him, molding her soft femininity over his hard male form.

She eased herself closer, knowing he was fighting to sustain their ecstasy as long as possible. "Matt," she whispered, hovering near his lips, "I want you more than I've ever wanted any man."

Her unrestrained admission inflamed him even more. "We can forget our pasts together, Kaye, forever," he rasped with effort. His hips began a slow, pulsating gyration, as ancient as time itself. He soared with desire and the knowledge that, at the moment, Kaye had forgotten her past. She was intent on enjoying the present to the fullest. And so was he.

Kaye's lips clasped his in a fierce kiss, and she matched his motions with erotic movements of her own. His hands traveled lingeringly down the shape of her firm back, her narrow waist, her rounded hips. When they dug into her flesh, pressing brazenly, she gasped audibly.

"Take me! Make me yours, Matt—" She thrust her taut, swollen breasts against his heated flesh and arched furiously with him. And they swayed together in tune to their own rhapsody.

In the wild eruption that followed, Matt's tortured voice rasped, "I love you, Kaye . . . love you!"

They rose together in flames of frenzied ecstasy, each freed from the past and consumed with the fires of the present. In timeless rapture, they clamored for each other, heated passion melding them together as one.

Finally, the flames died to glowing embers and they relaxed, cuddling exhaustedly. Tired, satisfied, completely fulfilled, they wrapped themselves in each other's arms and love. Matt gathered Kaye to him tenderly, rolling her to nestle against him. She smiled her contentment and dozed against the comfort of his arm and chest.

Some time later, Matt reached to switch off the light, then curled Kaye's nude form to his. He lay awake for a while, his thoughts roving to areas she had succeeded in making him forget—temporarily.

She stirred against him.

"Kaye? You awake?"

"Hmmm?" She hooked a slick leg over his rough hairy one.

"You know I can't stay here in Twin Oaks now that I've lost the election. I've got to get away. I love you, Kaye. Will you come with me?"

"Hmmm . . ." she mumbled again. He could feel her rhythmic breathing against his chest. It was then that he realized she had been asleep all along and not heard a thing he'd said. Well, he'd explain tomorrow. She would understand his position—and go with him.

The next day, Kaye listened quietly. But she did not go with him. She couldn't, and be true to herself. By evening, he was gone, and she was alone.

CHAPTER TEN

In the month following the election, Kaye kept very busy. Christmas was approaching and her antique business was brisk. The shop had even attracted a few clients from Dallas. They loved the old-fashioned friendly atmosphere as Kaye offered tea or coffee to her customers. Then, too, there were "finds" in Ye Olde Antique Shoppe not available in other local stores. The stock obtained in Delaware was so popular that Kaye considered another buying trip back East; perhaps after Christmas. Yes, she often acknowledged to herself, the shop was a tremendous source of pride. It was enabling her to be independent, and she threw herself into her work, *especially now that Matt was gone.*

She shuddered. Why did thoughts of him keep creeping up? She stacked the last dish on the drainboard and glanced out at the dreary December day. Thinking that hot tea was in order, she refilled the ever-simmering kettle and replaced it on the stove. Thank goodness, the day was almost over. She hated Sundays, because she didn't open the shop. She spent the morning cleaning her little farm-

165

house, the afternoon doing the books, and the evening
. . . *thinking about him.*

With a groan, Kaye curled up on the sofa and pulled the
warmth of the handmade afghan around her. Oh, she
clung to hope for a while. Finally, though, she realized
Matt wasn't returning to Twin Oaks, or to her. As he had
explained, there was nothing in the small town for him,
now that the mayoral race was out of the way.

Their final scene haunted her, and she regretted every
word. There were times when she wanted to drop everything and run to him. Most of the time, however, she
admitted that was impossible. Why didn't he come back
to her? Kaye realized that was unlikely.

They had met and laughed and loved, and now were
two people headed in different directions. It had been
wonderful while it lasted. But, was it *love?* Kaye still
questioned herself. She had been vulnerable and was swept
off her feet by Matt Logan's appealing masculinity and
delightful humor. Had she just been a challenge and—she
hated the thought—convenient for him?

And yet, he had declared his love . . .

"I want you with me, Kaye. *I love you!* Let's go to
Galveston or Corpus. I've just got to get out of here!" His
image loomed before her.

Love? If he loved her, he would understand why she
couldn't just leave home and business. She was settled. She
had "found herself." He was still searching. Her answer
was hollow: "My future is here."

His reply was somewhat irrational, but emphatic:
"Well, mine isn't! I can't stay here another day. My work
in Twin Oaks is finished. You knew that when I lost the
election. Let's go away together. Kaye, I'll take care of
you. Come with me."

Take care of you. She stiffened at the words and turned
her stricken face to him. "Don't you understand that I'm

166

independent for the first time in my life? I can't just leave my business a month after I've opened it!"

His blue eyes bore into her. "Do you mean you'd stay with that goddamn business rather than go with me?"

"Matt! It's not that simple!"

"Why not?"

Tears filled her large brown eyes. "Don't push me to a decision like that right now."

"Do you love me?" His words still rocked her.

She turned away, for she couldn't bear the look on his face. "I . . . I don't know."

His hand touched her shoulder, and she trembled. "Didn't all that we shared mean anything to you?"

"You know it did," she admitted thickly. "Matt, I can't fold up my new life and go with you, any more than you can stay here in this town. Don't you see where we are?"

He bowed his head and mumbled heavily, "Yeah, I see . . ."

With labored effort, Matt drew her to him, pressing her to his chest so that she could feel his heart reverberating through her body. He kissed her neck tenderly. "I'll be back, Kaye," he whispered huskily. His lips erased the salty trails on her cheeks . . .

Fresh tears flowed, and Kaye buried her face in the colorful afghan. Matt had taught her to love again . . . joyously and completely, and she missed him terribly. She had loved him. Oh, God, how she had loved him! But she had denied it, to them both, simply by refusing to go along. Was he really asking too much? Was she being unreasonable? Kaye only knew that since the day Matt left, her life had been hollow and empty.

She sighed shakily, trying to curb the tears. Oh, he had called. First, from Houston, she could hear boisterous noise in the background. A party, probably. Afterward, she had receded into her own quiet, morose world.

167

From Galveston, he called to say the weather was nice. The next week, Kaye plodded through cold, east Texas rain and poured herself into the job. She would have become completely secluded if Nan and Davis hadn't insisted that she spend Thanksgiving Day with their family.

Then came wind of fresh political activity for Matt, this time on the state level. Just last week, he called from Dallas to discuss his decision to run for the State House of Representatives. Would she join his campaign?

And his bed? she thought bitterly. She remembered her strained reply. "No! I won't follow you around from hotel to hotel, Matt! I have my own business, my own life! Please leave me alone. I'm happy here!" Kaye hated herself for the lies. And yet, she couldn't set herself up for this pain again.

Kaye hadn't heard from Matt since her outburst. She knew it was over between them. They couldn't even talk anymore. There was no communication nor understanding. Their goals were different. She had told him that when they first met. He wanted someone to warm his bed, whereas she sought independence and security. In retrospect, it seemed she was right from the beginning.

Kaye gazed blankly into the empty fireplace. Damn him! Damn Matt Logan! She hadn't come to Texas to fall in love. She came to build a new life for herself. Amazingly, she was doing it. Her antique business was growing. It didn't take the place of Matt's love, but maybe if she worked harder, she could forget him. Maybe . . .

The noise of a car in the driveway jolted her back to reality and the cold, dark room. Her face must be a wreck after all the self-pitying sobbing she had done! Kaye scrambled to the bathroom to splash cold water on her face before greeting whoever was there.

Heidi started her usual barking, but hushed prior to Kaye's return to the room. With the sudden quiet of the dog, Kaye knew it had to be someone familiar . . . perhaps Matt?

A quick staccato knock on the back door was followed by the sound of the door opening. Kaye's heart pounded, not from fear.

A female voice echoed through the darkness. "Kaye? Anybody home?"

"Oh, Nan! Come on in!" Kaye tried not to show the disappointment in her voice. "Let me get the light."

"Hi, Kaye. I just stopped by to see how you're doing," Nan commented almost flippantly. She stooped to talk with Heidi. "How's my favorite shepherd puppy? Is Kaye treating you okay, Heidi? Taking you for nice long walks so you can chase the little bunnies and get cockles in your fur?"

"How about a cup of coffee, Nan?" Kaye laughed at Nan's confidences with the animal as Heidi circled excitedly with the sudden attention she was receiving.

"Coffee sounds great. It'll help knock this chill. Kaye, it's cold in here. Didn't you notice?"

"I guess it is. I'll check the thermostat." Kaye nodded absently.

Nan joined her in the kitchen. "Heidi is a wonderful dog, Kaye."

Kaye raised her eyebrows. "There have been times when I would have cheerfully given her away. One day last week she accidentally skidded in the mud, then decided it was fun and rolled in it! I was an hour late opening the shop. And, of course, you remember the day she chased the skunk—and caught it!"

"Do I ever!" Nan laughed. She sat at the table and laid aside the newspaper she carried. Then, her voice grew serious. "Kaye, how are you? I've only seen you in passing the last few weeks."

Kaye poured instant coffee for Nan and tea for herself.

Joining Nan at the table, she smiled. "I'm busy. The shop is just keeping me totally occupied. What have you got there?"

Nan stirred her coffee, but didn't attempt to pick up the paper. "Your new ad will be in tomorrow's paper. Davis stopped by this evening and picked up a tearsheet so you could preview it."

"Well, let's see it!" Kaye's face lit up with the prospect of something new for the business.

Nan ignored the request and kept her elbow firmly on the paper. "You know, Kaye, maybe we should put an ad in one of the Dallas papers, perhaps on Sundays. Do you think it would cost much?"

Kaye eyed her friend. "Probably. Could we take a look at the ad?"

"The ad? Oh, it's just great." Nan leaned closer. "Kaye, uh, I know you've been extremely busy lately, and uh, well, how are you . . . really, now that Matt's gone."

Kaye blinked at the stark question. "Well, I'm, uh, staying busy and . . . I'm just fine."

"You don't look 'just fine.' You look like hell!"

Kaye looked away angrily. "Thanks a lot, Nan."

"Kaye, honey, I'm concerned about you. I want to help. Is there anything I can do? I know you must be hurting inside."

Kaye shook her head. "There's nothing you can do. In fact, there's nothing anyone can do."

"I'm worried about you, Kaye. Why don't you take a little break? I'll watch the shop while you go away for a few days."

"Leave the business? I can't do that!" The shop was the only thing keeping her from going crazy! Didn't Nan realize that?

"Take a few days and go talk to Matt. Go after him, Kaye," Nan urged.

Kaye looked across the table in amazement. "Go after Matt? It's too late, Nan. Whatever was between us is completely gone. It's over." She smiled resignedly, pleased that she could explain her personal calamity so pragmatically.

"You're telling me you don't love him?"

Kaye gritted her teeth. "I'm saying he doesn't love me. And the feeling is mutual. Now, could we talk about something else? How about that ad?"

Nan's hands slowly unfolded the newspaper. "That's why I came over to show it to you, Kaye. I wanted to prepare you . . . to be here when you saw it."

"Prepare me? Isn't the ad right? Did they mess it up?"

"No."

"Then, what?" Nan had acted strangely all evening, and Kaye had the feeling all along that there was something behind it.

"There is also a picture of Matt in the paper."

Kaye forced an immediate smile. "Well, I'm not surprised, Nan. He's getting his new campaign off the ground, you know."

"But, Kaye . . ."

Kaye reached impatiently for the paper. "My only concern is the advertisement for my store."

Nan bit her lip and thumbed to the second page, shoving it across the table to Kaye. There was the ad for Ye Olde Antique Shoppe all right. It was perfect, just as she had approved. Next to the ad was a picture of Matt Logan, candidate for the state legislature. Kaye's heart leaped to her throat as she read the caption. *Matt Logan and beautiful ex-wife patch differences for campaign trail.* Matt's arm encircled the shoulder of a smiling blond woman beside him. Neither the powerful image of Matt, nor his hand on her shoulder, bothered Kaye as much as that triumphant

171

smile on the face of the beautiful woman by his side. She had him back! Kaye could see it in her face!

Kaye looked away quickly, struggling to compose herself.

Nan's gentle voice penetrated the fog. "I hated for you to see this alone." She knew Kaye was still in love with him, no matter what she said. And it was obvious that she was in pain.

"Thank you, Nan. But, I'm a big girl and—" Her voice caught, and she rose to seek the dark solace of the adjoining den.

Nan followed her. "Kaye, the article is wrong. I don't believe Matt is reuniting with his wife. I know he doesn't love her. You know it, too."

Kaye laughed sarcastically and tried to be glib. "I guess they just happened to pass on the street at the same time some photographer snapped their gleaming smiles just before they chose the same car! All of it quite by chance, of course! And they rode off into the sunset together, happily ever—"

"Kaye! Stop it!"

"I'm sorry, Nan. I guess I am a little bitter. And upset. But I'll get over it. I always do . . ."

Nan's arm braced around her friend. "I feel somewhat responsible, Kaye. If it wasn't for me, you two would never have been thrown together. I didn't know he would be such a . . . a jackass! I had no idea he would leave."

Kaye shook her head stubbornly. "No, Nan. Matt and I were drawn together, not thrown. We're both completely responsible. I won't let you take that blame."

"Kaye, you're wonderful," Nan sighed with a tight smile. "I really need to go now. Are you sure you're all right?"

"You're a good friend, Nan. Don't worry about me. I'm fine. And . . . thanks."

172

Nan gave her a quick, affectionate hug before leaving. "See ya."

Kaye closed the door and leaned her forehead against it. With eyes squeezed tight, she tried to block out the photo, the proud smile on the woman's face, the possessive angle of Matt's arm around her. Oh, how Kaye hated her—and him!

How could you do this to me, Matt? If you loved me . . . if . . .

The little bell attached to the door of Ye Olde Antique Shoppe rang merrily as Gil Ashland entered. "Good morning, Kaye! How are you this cold winter Monday?"

Kaye looked up from her year-end inventory list and managed a smile. "I'm fine, Gil. How about you?" It was a trite answer that rolled easily off her tongue.

"Now that I've seen your radiance"—he crossed the length of the store—"my spirits are lifted. Your beautiful smile brightens this dreary morning for me."

What about my radiant red eyes? she thought acidly. "Flattery will get you nowhere, Gil. There aren't any giveaways in here. But you might be able to mooch a doughnut from Ella's Bakery down the street," she quipped.

"Ah, your sense of humor delights me, Kaye. I've already been to the bakery and"—he produced a small bag—"brought you a croissant to enjoy with your tea."

Her chestnut eyes lit on the golden pastry, and she smiled, in spite of herself. "Oh, Gil, you remembered how I love raisin croissants!" Eagerly she folded her books and hurried to prepare two cups of tea. The lovely French pastry was a delicacy too savory to pass.

"Remember? Oh, I recall every detail you ever mentioned to me, Kaye. Everything about you is imprinted on

173

my mind. How could I forget? Your beautiful hair, those dark eyes, your ruby lips . . . they haunt me at night."

She gave him a placating smile as she set the steaming cups before them. "Enough blarney, please!"

"Oh, I'm serious, my dear. I'm just a man, and you're very attractive. Kaye, you and I are on a different plateau than most people in this town. I think that's stimulating. We have some special interests in common, and should take advantage of them." His spoon circled the teacup slowly.

Kaye munched the delicate roll. "Like what?"

He cleared his throat. "Well, I like to participate in activities with people who appreciate the arts and fully enjoy the culture around us."

"Culture? Here in Twin Oaks?" She popped the crusty end of the roll into her mouth, relishing it to the fullest.

He took a sip of tea and measured his words. "No, Kaye. Not here. In Houston, or Galveston, or even San Antonio. Next week, I have business in Houston. How would you like to go along? We could tour the old homes in Galveston. Have you ever heard of the Bishop's Palace? It's filled with gorgeous antiques. You would love it."

She paused, midbite. "Go to Houston with you?"

He nodded. "Just the two of us . . ."

Recognition hit her with a thud. "Gil, you are a married man, and—"

He interrupted. "Kaye, it would be very discreet, I can assure you. No one would ever know. Wouldn't you like a little vacation on Galveston Beach?"

She shook her head. "I . . . I can't do that, Gil."

He held up his hand to stop her again. His voice was low, almost a whisper. "Don't make a decision now, Kathryn. Think about it."

"Gil, I don't vacation with married men."

174

"Kaye, Lillian is just a figurehead wife. We do not share a marital bed." His voice was urgent.

Bluntly Kaye asserted, "Well, don't look for me to solve your sexual problems, Gil."

His face grew red beneath his shock of white hair. "I thought I explained my feelings toward you, Kaye. We share a special kinship. I could introduce you to some culture, quality entertainment, the arts."

"And sexual fulfillment," she finished sarcastically. "Introduce them to someone else."

"Kaye," he sputtered, growing angry. "I'd advise you to think seriously about my offer."

"I've already thought about it, Gil. And the answer is no." Her voice was hard.

"Kaye, you're a very classy woman. You captured me from the moment I first saw you. I can understand your refusal this first time. But the offer remains open. Think about it."

"Gil, forget about me. I'm not available to you. I . . . my interest is elsewhere."

His vicious eyes cut into her. "Well, my dear, if you're referring to Matt Logan, he's gone. And you may as well forget about him, from the rumors I hear. He rushed back to the open arms of his ex-wife. You can bet there will be another wedding for them soon. Logan owes that much to his father-in-law for accepting money to finance the campaign."

Kaye was shaken by the news about Matt, but held her ground. "Gil, I am not interested in you, or any other married man. Is that clear?"

He assessed her slowly and answered in precise, clipped words. "Yes, Kaye, but I don't think you understand the implications of this refusal. Your business is at stake here."

Kaye stared at him. The audacity of the man and his

proposal didn't shock her half as much as his claim that Matt's campaign was being financed by his former father-in-law. No wonder his ex-wife wore a smile of proud possession! Financial involvement sealed the rift between her and Matt. If not love, then money would suffice! Damn!

"You would find our relationship rewarding. I'm looking for more than a bed partner. It could be very nice for you, Kaye. I would take care of you in many ways."

"Take care of me?" she shrilled. "I know exactly what you're looking for, and I can't help you! I won't!"

His lips hardened. "Is it worth saving your business?"

"You can't evict me! I have a year's lease in this building!"

He shrugged. "I can't help it, Kaye. I have someone who's offering twice the rent you are paying. It's simple business. I'm not evicting you, my dear. I'm only exercising my option on the lease."

"Option?" Kaye felt as though she was caught in an eddy.

He smiled shrewdly. "Certainly. There's a thirty-day option clause, and you signed it, my dear. Didn't you read the fine print?"

"I trusted you!" she muttered between clenched teeth.

Gil stood and met her gaze levelly. "Of course, if you should change your mind . . ."

Kaye leaned closer to his face and marshaled harshly, "Gil Ashland, you go to hell!"

He wheeled around and left her shop, ringing the little bell on the door merrily.

With a terrible sinking feeling, Kaye watched his figure disappear. She was drowning in that eddy. In thirty days her precious, growing business would fold, and her new life along with it.

* * *

Late that night, she picked up the phone and dialed with shaky fingers. The connection clicked distantly. Finally, a rather groggy voice answered.

"Hal?"

"Yes." His voice was low and sleepy. "Who is this . . . Kathryn?"

She smiled with the reassurance of his familiar voice. "Sorry I woke you, Hal. I can never keep the time difference straight."

He sensed something in her voice. "Kathryn, are you all right?"

"I'm fine," she rasped. "Are you . . . free next weekend?"

"Always, for you."

"Could you . . . come to Texas?" She choked back a sob.

"You know I'll be there." He was the same dear Hal.

CHAPTER ELEVEN

"Ye Olde Antique Shoppe . . . may I help you?"

"Nan? Nan—is that you?" Matt's voice boomed through the static, long-distance connection.

"Matt, what a nice surprise! How in the world are you? And how's the campaign going?" Nan smiled, hoping his call meant reconciliation with Kaye.

"I'm fine. How are you and Davis?" His voice sounded hollow and distant.

"We're still the same. When are you coming to visit? We'd love to see you!"

"Oh, don't know. I'm pretty busy these days. Is Kaye at the shop? Could I speak to her?" An urgency filled his tone.

"Matt, I'm sorry she's not here."

There was a pause, and his words were measured. "Well, where the hell is she? I've been trying to reach her."

"She'll be back tomorrow, Matt," Nan explained.

"Where is she now?" He paused, then, "Did she go back to Delaware?"

Nan was beginning to feel trapped. "No."

"Then, where the hell is she? Nan, talk to me! I need to reach her."

"Matt, I don't know if I should—"

"Nan, for God's sake!" Static punctuated his words.

"All right! She's gone to Dallas for the weekend."

"To Dallas? On a buying trip?"

"No. She's . . . oh, hell, Matt! She's meeting her old friend from Delaware, the man called Hal."

Matt's voice was suddenly strained. "Oh. That's all I need to know, Nan."

"Matt, why don't you come down here next week and talk to her. She needs you." Nan caught her breath, wondering if she had said too much.

"Thanks, Nan. But she doesn't need me. She has Hal."

"Matt, you're—" More static.

"Have a Merry Christmas, Nan. I'll see you when I can." The phone clicked.

Nan stood holding the receiver, feeling she had said all the wrong things. She shouldn't have mentioned Hal's name to Matt. *Oh, damn!* she thought miserably.

The waiter refilled their wineglasses and cleared away dinner plates. "Coffee, sir?"

"No, thanks." Hal waved him away impatiently. "Kathryn, I can't believe everything is as smooth as you say. You're as nervous as a cat." Hal leaned toward Kaye and examined her pale, thin face.

"Please, believe me. I'm just working too hard lately." Kaye nervously fingered her wineglass.

"Why did you call me, Kathryn? You were very upset that night."

She smiled. "What do you remember? You were half-asleep!"

His clear blue eyes flickered over her. "I remember."

Kaye gazed at Hal, so handsome and capable. He knew her well. She had intended throwing herself into his arms and pouring out her heart to him. She was prepared to tell him, embarrassing as it might be, of her affair with Matt Logan, ex-football star. Hal would understand. And yet, she held back. She spread her hands, hoping to convince him. "I just needed to see you, Hal. The holidays are here and . . ." Christmas carols filled the background, and candles flickered merrily on the tables. But Kaye's eyes reflected none of the holiday cheer.

"I would do anything for you, Kathryn. Surely you know that by now."

Her eyes softened. "I know."

His voice lowered. "Do you need money? You know it's not unusual at all for a new business such as yours to be overextended in the beginning months. I'll be glad to help you get your books in order or even to loan you enough cash to get straightened out. You're not too proud to ask me for money, are you, Kathryn?"

"Of course not." She smiled at his generous offer. "Financially, the business is showing a definite profit."

"What, then?"

Kaye's eyes traveled to Hal's stern, handsome face. What was wrong with her? Now was the time to explain that in less than a month, her valuable antique business would be out on the street. But she just couldn't tell him. "I know you won't understand this, Hal. But I needed you when I called. Now, I—" She paused and took a deep breath.

"Don't need me anymore?"

"No, it's just—"

"Well, Kathryn, I need you. And I want you. Tonight." His blue eyes settled on her honestly.

Kaye's brown eyes widened and met his.

"Yes, Kathryn. I want to spend the night with you. We

180

can deal with the rest later. I will take care of any problems you have."

Her dark eyes implored. "I . . . I can't do that, Hal."

His lips thinned. "I came all the way from Delaware to help you. I love you, Kathryn."

"Oh, Hal, I'm sorry—"

"It's not an affair I'm looking for. I want you to marry me, Kathryn."

Her head reeled as she realized she had led him to believe that was what she wanted, too. After all, she had asked him to come to her! "I can't," she grated morosely.

"Why?" He was pushing her.

Her mouth was dry. "Because I don't love you, Hal. I love . . . someone else."

"Then why did you call me?"

"I guess I didn't know, for sure, until we were together again. Until now. I'm sorry I called. Sorry I hurt you, Hal. I won't hurt you more by marrying you. It wouldn't be fair to either of us."

He ran his hand over his face. "This isn't what I expected. I don't know what to say—"

Kaye placed her napkin on the table. "Don't even try, Hal. I'm sorry it didn't work out." Kaye was amazed at her own calmness. She stood up. "I'll drive you back to the hotel. Then I'm going home."

Moist diamonds sparkled over the backyard as the early-morning sun touched dew-laden grass. Heidi frisked happily, sniffing curiously at everything.

Kaye stood on the small brick patio and absently watched her frosty breath. She hated what had happened last night with Hal. She hadn't slept much, thinking about their exchange and—oh, God!—his defeated expression when he heard that she didn't love him. She knew now she would never marry Hal. And she had finally admitted the truth about her love for Matt.

Because of that love, she now had to face her life and problems alone. She couldn't ask Hal for help. She honestly couldn't face him again, knowing of his love for her and how much it hurt him that she didn't return that love. She didn't want to hurt him anymore, and the only way to avoid that was to walk away, as hard as it was. A sob welled up inside her as she remembered her deliberate act.

Now, however, she had to decide what to do about her business. Damn Gil Ashland! Matt was right about him! He had this town, and her, right in his palm! Well, maybe she could rent an old farmhouse or something. Kaye sighed, thinking how much work it would entail.

And she wouldn't have Matt to help her this time. He was back in the arms of . . . Kaye shuddered, unable to bear the thoughts.

Kaye hugged herself and urged Heidi to hurry. Thoughts of Matt sent tingles down her spine. She longed for his smile, ached for his arms around her.

Suddenly Heidi lifted her head, ears alert. The pup's barrage of barking warned her of an approaching vehicle in the driveway. Then, just as abruptly, Heidi hushed and ran to greet the newcomer.

Kaye held her breath and stood rooted to the spot. There were only a few people that Heidi greeted affectionately. Nan, Davis or . . . Matt. *Matt!*

She swallowed hard and waited. It was *Matt*, she just knew! And then, he rounded the corner of the house—big and bold and oh, so handsome. He appeared blonder or thinner or somehow different than she remembered when she held him close. That time seemed eons ago as they stared at each other across the early-morning chill.

Matt stood very still for a moment, taking in her natural

beauty—the tumbled, auburn hair, her deep-set mahogany eyes, the slightly parted lips—God! He had missed her!

Kaye spoke first, her voice straining for audibility. "The most logical question is, what are you doing here at this time of the morning?"

He shrugged, sounding almost casual. "I needed to get away from the campaign. Thought I'd go fishing with Davis. When I saw your light, I couldn't pass your house without stopping."

"Haven't I heard that line before?"

He closed the space between them, a half-grin tugging at his lips. "Seems like déjà vu, pretty lady. We've got to stop meeting like this . . ." He paused until her smile joined his teasing grin. "There! That's the smile I've missed."

Kaye's heart fluttered helplessly as he breathed his old favorite nickname for her. How many times had he called her that when life and love came easier for them both? "These odd-hour meetings do seem to be a habit of yours —ours," she amended, recalling that first early-morning visit last fall when he had insisted on including himself in her life. And she had eagerly welcomed him. Her dark brown eyes met his intense blue ones. "You are the only man I know who chooses such an unconventional rendezvous, Matt."

He touched her arm, and Kaye felt his warm radiance surging through their connection. "You're cold. Could we go inside?"

She was drawn by Matt's magnetism and wanted to reach up and clasp him to her. An involuntary shudder rippled over her as she refrained, "Would you like a cup of hot tea?" It was a repeat of the previous scene—same corny jokes, same time and place, same offer of tea. For a crazy moment, Kaye considered pinching herself to see if all this was real. Maybe her imagination had gone wild!

No, if it's a dream, I don't want to destroy the illusion of having Matt with me again. Even if he's only temporary.

"Hot tea sounds fine," he agreed, following her into the kitchen.

Kaye moved through the kitchen, her silky robe flapping around her ankles. Matt watched her hungrily as the robe parted occasionally to reveal a long, smooth leg. She wedged porcelain cups in saucers, trying not to show her nervousness. When the teakettle whistled, she grabbed it quickly and poured the steamy liquid into their cups.

Matt broke the heavy silence. "I thought you were spending the weekend with Hal."

She raised startled eyes to him. "How did you know that?"

"Nan told me. I've been trying to get in touch with you."

She folded her arms over tightly outlined breasts. "Well, well, Nan is quite informative, isn't she?"

"Don't drag Nan into this. I insisted on knowing. Now I almost wish I hadn't. Are you packing to move back to Delaware?"

"No," she answered indignantly. "My home is here. Or have you forgotten?"

"Does that mean you aren't going back with Hal?"

Kaye took a sip of tea to prolong her answer. "It means that I won't be going with Hal at all. You see"—she took a deep breath—"I made the mistake of falling in love with the mayoral candidate in this little one-horse town. When he lost the election, he left me high and dry, as they say in Texas."

By the time the words were out, Matt had gripped her forearms and lifted her off the chair. Close to her nose, he muttered, "What did you say?"

Tears were dangerously close to the edge, but she countered him adamantly. "I said I was fool enough to fall in love with you!"

"Kaye . . . oh, Kaye, I can't believe you're finally admitting it!" His lips claimed her, and he crushed her against his chest. She allowed herself to be drawn into Matt's warmth, relishing the power of his rock-hard muscles around her. It felt so wonderful to be in his arms once again, tasting his lips, feeling his heart throbbing against her breasts, knowing the unleashed male strength molded to her tight body. She never wanted this dream to end as she was swept into the ecstasy of Matt's dynamic energy.

"Matt—" she whimpered, impotently pushing herself from his fierce grasp. Suddenly, she remembered he belonged to another woman. "Matt, please, don't!"

"Kaye, I've waited months to hear you say that you loved me! Don't push me away now!" He was nibbling crazily at her ear and neck.

"I . . . I know about you and your former wife. I have no intention—"

"What in hell are you talking about?" he demanded harshly, listening to her again.

"Your ex-wife," she tried to explain breathlessly. "You've been seen together. And the rumor is that you'll remarry. I know her father is financing your campaign."

"I am not remarrying Megan! Where did you get such a preposterous idea?"

She shrugged, confused, and he went on. "True, her father is supplying some of the financial backing for the campaign. We happen to be good friends, and he believes in me. But remarriage to his daughter is not a factor. I wouldn't marry her again for all the oil in Texas! I love you, Kaye! I love you so much I can't stand to be apart from you another day!"

"Then, you're not getting married?" She leaned weakly

185

against him, feeling somewhat dizzy with the speedy turn of events.

"Only to you, my pretty lady. As soon as we can!"

Her arms inched around his neck. "What? *What?* Married? Matt—are you sure?"

"I've never been more sure of anything in my life! I love you, Kaye Coleman! And I want you with me always."

"I want to be with you, too, but—"

"If you're worried about your business, maybe it's time we talked about incorporating that chain of antique stores."

"Yes," she agreed happily. "Maybe it is."

"We'll move the home office to Dallas, along with the chairwoman of the board!"

"Oh, Matt, you make everything sound so easy!" Kaye squeezed her arms around him tightly and he lifted her off the floor.

"I know one thing that's going to be so easy!" He whisked her up in his arms, cradling her against his chest. "Our loving will be easy! Oh, God, Kaye, I've missed you so!" He carried her into the bedroom.

"Matt, you'd better call Davis and cancel fishing."

"Cancel fishing?"

"Didn't you tell Davis you'd meet him this morning to go fishing?"

"Oh, that." He smiled sheepishly as he laid her gently on the bed. "Davis isn't really expecting me. I drove here to see if you had spent the night with Hal. I couldn't sleep for thinking of his hands on you!"

Her finger traced his nose and lips. "Matt, what if I hadn't been here."

He bent over her. "I would have camped on your doorstep until you returned. Then, I would have kidnapped you until you agreed to love me forever!" His lips nibbled along her jawline.

"I agree! I will love you forever!" She giggled as his lips tickled certain sensitive areas.

"That was easy enough! Now, let's see if I can persuade you to marry me!" His hands tore open her robe and his lips buried a kiss.

"I do, I do!" She laughed gaily and pulled him over her. "I do love you, Matt Logan! And I will marry you. And love you forever!"

"Wonder if Nan and Davis would like to have our wedding on their patio next weekend?" he mused as his tongue lit a flaming trail down her belly.

"Hmmm, how appropriate," Kaye smiled with delight. "And romantic. It's where we first met."

He paused. "Not quite."

She took his face in her hands and declared, "The first time we met was at the political rally at Chandlers."

He began to work at removing his shirt and slacks. "I have loved you since the moment I laid eyes on that gorgeous copper hair blowing from your recklessly speeding Corvette."

Her eyes narrowed. "What are you talking about?"

He eased his solid muscular body back into her arms. "You almost demolished my car the day you so carelessly breezed in town!"

"You?" she breathed incredulously. "That was your car?"

"Yes, pretty lady. I wanted you then. I want you now," he murmured, letting his lips play along her neck.

"If I'd only known!"

"If you had known I was after you from the start, you probably would have run like a scared rabbit."

She smiled perceptively. "I knew . . ."

"Then why didn't you run?"

She pulled his face close and kissed him longingly. "I

fell flat on my face, and you helped me up. And taught me to love and laugh again."

"I couldn't let you go . . ." His lips flamed her passions, and she responded eagerly.

"I'm glad," she sighed, molding herself even closer. "I love you, Matt . . ."